*A Parisian Bourgeois' Sundays
and Other Stories*

Also by Guy de Maupassant and translated by Marlo Johnston
Afloat: A Journal of His Days at Sea

A Parisian Bourgeois' Sundays and Other Stories

Guy de Maupassant

Translated from the French by Marlo Johnston

PETER OWEN
LONDON & CHESTER SPRINGS

PETER OWEN PUBLISHERS
73 Kenway Road London SW5 0RE

Peter Owen Books are distributed in the USA by
Dufour Editions Inc. Chester Springs PA 19425-0007

First published in Great Britain 1997
© Marlo Johnston 1997

ISBN 0 7206 1033 8

A catalogue record for this book is available from the British Library

Printed and made in Great Britain by Biddles of Guildford and King's Lynn

Contents

Introduction

Twelve of these fifteen stories have never before been published in English, one appeared once but is now hard to find, and in any case that and the remaining two have long been out of print.

In all, twenty-nine of Maupassant's stories have never been translated into English. They may have been overlooked because Maupassant himself did not collect them into a volume in his usual way. But this immediately raises the question: Why did he leave them in obscurity?

It was Maupassant's habit to publish his stories first in the press, most often in the newspapers *Le Gaulois* and *Gil Blas*, and then to collect a dozen or so into a volume, to be followed by further individual newspaper or magazine publications here and there, thus getting the maximum exposure from each story; but a number of stories made only their initial appearance, no doubt for a variety of reasons at which we can now only conjecture. Most of them were published in France a few years after his death, though a few long remained undiscovered.

Of those twenty-nine stories it has to be said that a few are frankly very poor and there was excellent reason for Maupassant to leave them alone, but those are the minority. He reused parts of others, but this in itself is not a reason to withhold them as he constantly reused and revised stories or parts of them. Only when they reappeared almost in their entirety, as did the two used *en bloc* in the book *Sur l'eau* (in English translation *Afloat*, Peter Owen, 1995), could this explain why the originals did not reappear. Some were quite slight preparatory sketches for a later, longer work, and it is not surprising that the original was allowed to disappear (though it may be of interest now). Sometimes the only discernible reason is that they seem to have an extremely personal slant, verging on the autobiographical. Some seem to be as much article as story, and Maupassant never collected his articles into a book. Yet for some stories none of this will do and neglect seems almost inexplicable.

It has been said rather dismissively that some of the untranslated stories are 'early work'. The present selection does in fact come mainly from the first half of Maupassant's ten-year productive period, but they were also all published after 'Boule de suif', and no one has ever suggested that to be 'early', and still less to be inadequate. Maupassant's really early work came before he became famous almost overnight with 'Boule de suif' in 1880; six stories published before that are known, and one other remained unpublished.

For all that, 'A Parisian Bourgeois' Sundays' (1880) may in fact have been partly written some time before 1880, since Maupassant wrote to his mother on 6 October 1875 that as soon as he finished the play he was writing he would start a series of stories called *Grandes Misères des petites gens*, and he already had six subjects for it. No other series fitting this title is known; if he did start it then, some of it would have been written at a time when Flaubert was greatly influencing Maupassant's writing, and also discouraging him from too early publication.

A possible inspiration for these stories is the children's song 'Bon voyage, Monsieur Dumollet', for Monsieur Dumollet, like Monsieur Patissot, goes on journeys and they share the attributes of good sense allied with a certain naivety; and Maupassant mentions Monsieur Dumollet in Part II, 'First outing', in a quotation also used by Flaubert. It is also possible that the series was a combination of the early stories about the great misery of humble workers in ministerial offices (a subject close to Maupassant's heart!) and Monsieur Dumollet's travels. There are also echoes, originally almost certainly unconscious, of Flaubert's characters Bouvard and Pecuchet, but Maupassant may only later have realized this; some months after the Monsieur Patissot series had appeared Maupassant acquired close knowledge of *Bouvard et Pecuchet* as he was asked by Flaubert's niece to attempt to complete the unfinished work from Flaubert's copious documentation.

Other parts of the series came about in different ways. Some were written in 1880 at the request of his editor, for instance, Part V about Zola's house, clearly contemporary as it reflected the progress of Zola's building project, and the feminist meeting of Part X, which was based by Maupassant on gatherings held at the time and which, to judge by other press comments, he in no way exaggerated.

There is also a good deal of discreet autobiography in these stories; Maupassant had spent his own Sundays in the same area as Monsieur Patissot when he was a Ministry clerk, and he rented rooms at Sartrouville during the summer of 1880. He did very similar things – walking, fishing, above all rowing, and much more besides – and certainly with rather greater verve than Monsieur Patissot. He also made use of his experiences at the Marine Ministry and showed many colleagues in a rather unflattering light; he had asked Zola's permission to include him, but it is very doubtful if anyone else was similarly privileged.

There are multiple autobiographical elements in Part VII, 'A Sad Story'. Maupassant himself was brought up at Etretat, had lessons from the *curé* there and was then sent to school at Yvetot, of which he paints an accurate picture; he also had a younger brother, but six years younger, and they had little in common. He has gone further back in family history, too: it was his maternal grandfather who on his father's death was left in the care of his uncle the *curé*, and he even mentions Darnetal, where that grandfather had a factory, but it was *his* father who had been a miller. Maupassant reworked and enlivened this story in 1883 as 'A Surprise', but curiously neither version was ever repeated or collected into a volume, perhaps because he saw them as too personal. He soon stopped putting such easily identifiable details in his work.

'A Page of Unpublished History' (1880) came about as the result of a holiday that year in Corsica, where Maupassant was told the story, which appears to be of events in 1793. At first sight it comes into the category of an article or historical document, but it was also certainly written as literature; in Napoleon's will the beneficiaries mentioned were spread over multiple codicils, but Maupassant reduced them to one to simplify the story. He wrote the whole thing to extract the maximum dramatic effect, despite his remark about not making it more 'literary' or more dramatic!

'Public Opinion' (1881) uses characters from Maupassant's time at the Marine Ministry, and also uses some of the names from 'A Parisian Bourgeois' Sundays', seeming almost like a continuation of it, but it is more of a satire on current affairs disguised as a story. The department store fire clearly dated it and made it difficult to reuse. It is worth knowing for Monsieur Rade alone who, though the name is the same, is nevertheless not entirely the Monsieur Rade of Monsieur Patissot's office, who in

that story may have been based on 'an old head clerk of bo-
hemian ways' in the Marine Ministry; he has become a much
younger man and is a journalist, though as in the earlier series
the political opinions he expresses so strongly bear more than a
passing resemblance to Maupassant's own.

'Recollection' (1882) draws on Maupassant's experience of
the retreat from Rouen in the Franco-Prussian war. He wrote
three similar stories using the same incident of the old man and
his daughter in 1878, 1882 and 1884. The first, 'Le Mariage du
Lieutenant Laré', is curiously anodyne, like two other stories
that appeared in *La Mosaïque*; it seems not to have been noticed
that this publication was subsidized by the Ministry of Fine Art
and Education (where Maupassant was working at the time)
and was intended for schools, so Maupassant was evidently
writing the three stories for a specific young market; it is not
surprising therefore that he left them dormant. The final version, 'Les Idées du colonel' (which was collected into a volume),
again has the same subject but is told by the now aged captain
as a recollection of his youth; 'Souvenir' is more vivid than the
first version and seems much fresher and closer to the partly
autobiographical experience than the third.

'Other Times' (1882) is half article and half story. At the time
it was written there was an uproar in the press about whether
the law should allow men to live off women, and students from
the Latin Quarter had taken direct action against some ponces;
Maupassant considers other aspects to the matter. He was regularly publishing both articles and stories in the same newspaper,
and comment on a news item, leading into a story, was a natural
and accepted practice.

'Yveline Samoris' (1882) is a short sketch for the novella
Yvette. It somehow seems much closer to the facts which

perhaps inspired it than the later work and, maybe because it is so short, has a more lively immediacy. This world of flashy foreigners was well known to Maupassant in his early years; though he was not a gambler many of his friends were, and he probably found a good many characters and stories in such salons.

It would be difficult to find a slighter work than 'The Cough' (1883), but it is none the less amusing for that. It is dedicated to, and perhaps a parody of, the Parnassian poet and art critic Armand Silvestre, who was best known for writing quite naturally and comically about natural functions. It was never collected into a volume by Maupassant or posthumously, and only in the 1950s was it discovered in *Panurge*, a short-lived publication of 1882 and 1883.

'A True-Life Drama' (1883), if it was true, may not have been published again for that very reason; it is written almost like an article. If it was not true, it is an ingenious story. The idea was later turned into a deathbed confession by a woman who had murdered her sister's fiancé, but there is otherwise no real resemblance between the two versions; this one, true or not, has passion, detective work and conflict of loyalties in addition, yet it is far neater.

'Advice Given in Vain' (1884) may demonstrate the effect of time on Maupassant's experience of clinging women. He wrote an article on the subject in 1881 when his solution to the problem was to keep them, to keep them all, yet three years later he considers poison! He is particularly outspoken here about older women, as with the character Madame Walter in his novel *Bel-Ami*, but he took much the same view of younger ones and was known to have used the disappearance method himself.

'Doctors and Patients' (1884) is set in the Auvergne where

Maupassant had been the previous year and which was to be the setting for his novel *Mont-Oriol* of 1885. Curiously, the part about the old man had been published on its own two years before, but Maupassant did not use either form again, although the old man is an amazing character.

'The Rondoli Sisters' (1884) was previously translated, but it has long been out of print; it is one of those stories which suffered from Anglo-Saxon prudery, and the correct words were never used to describe the Italian girl, nor was her particular animal sensuality shown as Maupassant intended. It is known that Maupassant visited Italy in 1885 and 1889, but there was little trace of his having been earlier. We now know that he visited his mother at Santa Margarita in 1881,* and several articles and stories mention a journey from Genoa to Marseille before he published 'The Rondoli Sisters', but if there is some autobiographical element in this story we are unlikely ever to know it.

The first passages of 'Letter from a Madman' (1885) show Maupassant's scientific curiosity in the workings of the senses, then a progression to the entirely supernatural. He was always deeply interested in the how and the why of any aspect of animal and human behaviour, and especially the eye as he himself had problems arising from syphilis affecting the optic nerve. He had also attended Charcot's lectures at the Salpetrière Hospital (as had Freud), and his thoughts on all these matters eventually led him from this story to 'Le Horla' (1887); the supernatural becomes more dominant in the progression of the three stories, 'Letter from a Madman', the first version of 'Le Horla' (1886) and the final well-known version.

---

*From her letter of 6 October 1881, *Maupassant inédite*, pp. 61–3; also Louis Forestier's article 'Maupassant et l'Italie', in *Maupassant multiple*, pp. 7–15.

In 'From Paris to Heyst' (1887) Maupassant was a historical witness of his period; it is an article, but it is written so dramatically, using all his literary talent, that it is also a good story. He was accused of making the ascent as publicity for 'Le Horla', and it may indeed have been useful in that respect, but it was obviously the experience itself that fascinated him.

'The Donkey' (1883) has long been out of print; Maupassant's animal stories seem to be unappreciated in English, perhaps because they are cruel. They are cited as proof of Maupassant's sadism, but it is often forgotten that in the nineteenth century cruelty to animals – and children for that matter – was routine and that Maupassant wrote of what he saw around him. It is quite clear where his sympathies lie, and he implicitly criticizes the cruelty by exposure.

Maupassant was often critical of the world he lived in, and evidence for this can be found everywhere in his writing, but it is not always appreciated. In *Bel-Ami* Maupassant was depicting the nineteenth-century version of the unacceptable face of capitalism, with its ally the unacceptable face of journalism, and he pulled no punches in his exposure; yet Henry James remarked that it was 'the story of a cad by a cad'. This sharp critical faculty is also present in this selection, though it is not dominant, perhaps just because many of the stories are early. They are a mixed bag of the untranslated, but they have certain things in common. Most of them cover the same geographical area, the same area painted by the Impressionists: Paris and especially the Seine west of Paris which Maupassant knew so well. He is well known for his tales of Normandy, but only two are set there, and one in each of the Auvergne, Corsica and Italy.

They also have in common his special kind of humour –

a sense of the comic irony of life. In 'A Parisian Bourgeois' Sundays' he sends up everyone, including Monsieur Patissot, quite outrageously but with affection and understanding. Maupassant was a satirist – it shows especially in his articles – and here his satirical eye fixes on flights of rhetoric, early feminism, bourgeois taste and, more gently, Zola's love of the grandiose, even to his dog.

Most of these stories were not chosen by Maupassant himself for further publication and were therefore not revised by him (he generally did this between newspaper and book publication). That may be precisely the reason they show a very little more of what he did not especially want revealed. He firmly believed that only his works belonged to the public, not his private life, and he meant to maintain a strict impersonality. For all his effort a good deal of the man comes through in everything he wrote, and perhaps a little more in these stories which had less later editing and so were less prepared. They, and he, are well worth getting to know.

A Parisian Bourgeois' Sundays

I
Travel preparations

Monsieur Patissot, who was born in Paris and had studied unsuccessfully like so many others at the Henri IV College, had gone into a Ministry thanks to the influence of one of his aunts, who kept the tobacconists where a divisional head bought his supplies.

He progressed very slowly, and might perhaps have died as a clerk in the fourth grade were it not for the benevolent chance which sometimes orders our destinies.

Today he is fifty-two, and it is only at this age that he is beginning to explore, like a tourist, the whole area of France that extends between the Paris fortifications and the provinces.

The story of his promotion may be useful to many employees, just as the account of his expeditions may be helpful to many Parisians, who may use them as an itinerary for their own excursions and thereby, thanks to his example, avoid certain misadventures which befell him.

In 1854 Monsieur Patissot was still earning only 1,800 francs. Owing to an unusual effect of his nature he was displeasing to all his superiors, who left him to languish, eternally and despairingly waiting for a rise, that ideal of the employee.

He worked nevertheless, but he did not know how to make it look as if he did, and then, as he would say, he was too proud. His pride amounted to never greeting his superiors in a base and obsequious manner, as in his opinion did certain of his colleagues, whom he would prefer not to name. He would add further that his frankness upset quite a few people, since he spoke out (as did everyone else, mind you) against unfair promotions, injustices and good turns done for outsiders who were nothing to do with the bureaucracy. But his indignant voice was never heard beyond the door of the cubicle where he toiled or, as he liked to say, 'I slave … in every sense, monsieur.'

First of all as an employee, then as a Frenchman, and finally as a man of order, he supported on principle every established government, since he was an enthusiastic upholder of power … apart from that of his bosses.

Whenever he could, he would position himself on the Emperor's route so as to have the honour of removing his hat, and off he would go filled with pride at having saluted the Head of State.

Through contemplating the Sovereign, he did as many do: he imitated him in the cut of his beard, the arrangement of his hair, the shape of his overcoat, his walk, his gestures. How many men, in every country, seem to be portraits of the prince! Perhaps he did bear a vague resemblance to Napoléon III, but his hair was black – so he dyed it. Then the likeness was total; and when he met another man in the street who also reproduced the imperial features he would be jealous and would look him over disdainfully. This need for imitation soon became his *idée fixe*, and having heard a bailiff from the Tuileries imitate the Emperor's voice, Patissot in turn took on his intonation and calculated slowness.

In this way he became so very like his model that you might have taken one for the other, and the people in the Ministry, the top civil servants, whispered to one another, finding it unseemly, even improper. Someone spoke about it to the Minister, who requested this employee to come and see him. But at the sight of him he began to laugh, and repeated two or three times, 'It's comic, really comic!' This was overheard, and the next day

Patissot's immediate superior put forward his subordinate's name for a rise of three hundred francs, which he got at once.

From that time he progressed in a regular fashion, thanks to this simian faculty for imitation. Even a vague unease came over his superiors, like the feeling of a great fortune suspended above your head, and they spoke to him with deference.

But when the Republic came it was a disaster for him. He felt finished, drowned and, losing his head, stopped dying his hair, shaved himself completely and had his hair cut short, thereby achieving a gentle and benevolent appearance which compromised him very little.

Then his superiors took revenge for the prolonged intimidation he had exercised over them and, all becoming republican from conservative instinct, they persecuted him through his bonuses and blocked his promotion. He, too, changed his opinions, but the Republic not being a palpable and living character which it was possible to resemble, and the presidents succeeding each other with rapidity, he found himself plunged into the most cruel embarrassment, in such terrible distress, impeded in his need to imitate, after the failure of an attempt at his most recent ideal, Monsieur Thiers.

Yet he needed a new manifestation of his personality. He sought for a long time; then one morning he presented himself in the office with a new hat which had as a cockade a very small tricolour rosette on the right side. His colleagues were dumbfounded; they laughed about it all day, and again the next day, and all week, for a month. But in the end the gravity of his attitude disconcerted them; and once more his superiors became uneasy. What mystery was this sign hiding? Was it a simple statement of patriotism? Was it a witness to his support of the Republic? Or perhaps the secret sign of some powerful affiliation? But then, to

wear it so determinedly, you would have to be very sure of powerful and hidden protection. In any event it would be wise to be on
guard, the more so because his imperturbable sang-froid at all the
joking increased their uneasiness even more. They spared him a
second time, and his simpleton's courage saved him, for he was at
last appointed senior clerk on 1 January 1880.

His whole life had been sedentary. He had remained a bache-
lor from a love of peace and tranquillity, for he detested movement and noise. His Sundays were generally spent in reading
adventure novels and in carefully arranging transparencies which
he would afterwards give to his colleagues. He had only had leave
three times in his life, on each occasion for a week, in order to
move house. But sometimes, when there was a big public holiday,
he would take an excursion train to Dieppe or Le Havre, so as to
elevate his soul with the imposing sight of the sea.

He was full of the kind of good sense that verges on stupidity.

He had lived for a long time peacefully, economically, being
prudently moderate, and in any case he was chaste by tempera-
ment, but then a terrible anxiety came over him. In the street one
evening, all of a sudden, he felt a giddiness which made him fear
an attack. He took himself off to a doctor and obtained from him,
for a hundred sous, this prescription:

> Monsieur X, fifty-two years, unmarried, employed. Sanguine
> type, risk of stroke. Cold water lotions, moderate nourishment,
> plenty of exercise.
>
> Montellier, MD, Paris.

Patissot was appalled, and for a month he spent the whole day in
his office with a moistened towel round his forehead, rolled like a
turban; drops of water would constantly fall on his work, which he

had to start again. Over and again he would re-read the prescription, no doubt in the hope of grasping some unnoticed meaning, of penetrating the doctor's secret thoughts and also of discovering what propitious exercise could really protect him from apoplexy.

So he consulted his friends, showing them the deadly paper. One of them advised boxing. He straight away sought out a teacher, and on the very first day took a straight punch on the nose which released him for ever from this healthy diversion. The singlestick made him gasp for breath, and he ached so much after fencing that he spent two nights without sleep. Then he saw the light. He would go on foot every Sunday to see the surroundings of Paris, and even parts of the capital that he did not know well.

How to equip himself for these journeys preoccupied him for a whole week, and on Sunday, the thirtieth day of May, he began his preparations.

After having read all the oddest advertisements, which poor wretches, one-eyed or lame, determinedly handed out on street corners, he went to the shops with the sole intention of looking around, saving the buying for later.

First he went to the premises of a so-called American boot-maker, asking to see some stout travelling shoes! He was shown a kind of appliance that was copper clad like a warship, bristling with nails like a steel harrow and made (he was assured) from bison leather from the Rocky Mountains. He was so enthusiastic that he would willingly have bought two pairs. One was enough, however. He contented himself with that, and he left, carrying them under his arm, which was soon numb.

He got some corduroy fatigue trousers, like the ones carpenters wear; then gaiters of oiled sailcloth which came up to the knees.

He still needed a soldier's knapsack for his provisions, a marine telescope to identify distant villages clinging to the hillsides, and finally an ordnance survey map, which would enable him to find his way without asking farm workers as they stooped low in the fields.

Then, the better to tolerate the heat, he decided to acquire a light alpaca garment which the famous firm of Raminau produced to the highest quality, according to its advertisements, for the modest sum of six francs fifty centimes.

He went to this establishment, and a tall, refined young man, hair cut *à la Capoul*,* pink nails like a lady and a constant smile, showed him the garment he asked for. It did not match the magnificence of the advertisement. So Patissot hesitantly asked, 'But will it do the job?' The other looked away with well-simulated embarrassment like an honest man who does not want to betray the client's trust and, lowering his voice with a hesitant air, 'Good lord, sir, you know that for six francs fifty you can't produce an article like this one, for example ...' And he produced a jacket noticeably better than the first. After examining it, Patissot asked the price. 'Twelve francs fifty.' It was tempting. But, before deciding, he once more questioned the tall young man, who was looking at him fixedly, observantly. 'And ... that's a good one? Do you guarantee it?' 'Oh, certainly, sir, it is excellent and it is flexible. Of course, you mustn't let it get wet! Oh, as good goes, it's good; but you know there's quality and quality. For the price, it's ideal. Twelve francs fifty, think of it, it's nothing. Certainly a jacket at twenty-five francs is better value. For twenty-five francs you get the very best; as strong as twill, even more durable. When there has been rain, a touch of the iron and it's good as new. The colour never changes, it doesn't redden in the sun. It is warmer and

---

* In the style of a popular singer of the time, parted in the middle with a curl each side coming on to the forehead.

lighter at the same time.' And he spread out his merchandise, made the material shimmer, crumpled it, shook it, spread it out to show off the excellent quality.

He was talking interminably, convincingly, dissipating hesitation with gesture and rhetoric.

Patissot was convinced; he bought it. The pleasant salesman tied the parcel with string, still talking, and up at the cash desk, near the door, he continued to praise the value of the purchase emphatically. When it was paid for, he suddenly fell silent; he bowed with an 'It's a pleasure, sir,' accompanied by a superior smile, and holding the door open he watched his client leaving, vainly trying to wave goodbye, both his hands laden with parcels.

Back at home, Monsieur Patissot studied his first itinerary carefully and wanted to try on his shoes, whose steel fittings created a kind of sled. He slipped on the floor, fell and made up his mind to be careful. Then he spread out all his purchases on the chairs and contemplated them at length. He went off to sleep thinking to himself: It's strange that I didn't think before about excursions to the countryside!

II
First outing

Monsieur Patissot worked badly all week at his Ministry. He was dreaming of the excursion planned for the following Sunday, and a great longing for the countryside came over him suddenly, a need to feel sentimental beneath the trees, a thirst for the pastoral ideal which haunts Parisians in springtime.

On Saturday he went to bed early, and as soon as it was day he was up.

His window opened on to a dark and narrow yard, a sort of chimney perpetually funnelling all the smells produced by poor households. At once he raised his eyes to the little square of sky that was showing between the roofs, and he made out a bit of deep blue, already full of sun, endlessly crossed by flights of swallows that could only be followed for a second. He said to himself that from up there they must be able to see the distant countryside, the green of the wooded hills, a whole array of horizons.

Then a confused desire came over him to lose himself amongst the freshness of the leaves. He quickly got dressed, put on his fear-some shoes and spent a very long time buckling his gaiters, which he was not at all used to. After loading on his back his bag stuffed with meat, bread, cheeses and bottles of wine (for the exercise would surely make him hungry), he set out, walking stick in hand.

He adopted a rhythmic marching stride (as hunters do, he thought), whistling lively tunes which made his pace lighter. People turned to look at him, a dog yapped; a passing coachman shouted to him, '*Bon voyage*, Monsieur Dumollet!'* But he didn't care a bit, and went on his way without turning round, ever faster, whirling his walking stick with a bold air.

The town was waking up joyfully, in the warmth and light of a beautiful spring day. The fronts of the houses were gleaming, the canaries were singing in their cages, and gaiety was running through the streets, lighting up the faces, spreading laughter everywhere, like a contentment with everything under the bright rising sun.

He was on his way to the Seine to take the packet boat which would drop him at Saint-Cloud. Amid the stupefaction of passers-by he followed the Rue de la Chaussée d'Antin, the Boulevard

---

* The title of a well-known song at the time of Louis-Philippe, caricaturing a typical bourgeois going on journeys armed with an umbrella; a version highly defamatory to Napoleon III and the Empress was current at the time of the Franco-Prussian war.

and the Rue Royale, comparing himself mentally to the Wandering Jew. As he mounted a pavement, the steel reinforcements of his shoes slipped once more on the granite, and he fell heavily, producing a terrible noise in his bag. Some passers-by helped him up, and he started walking again more gently, as far as the Seine, where he awaited a boat.

In the distance, far off under the bridges, he could see it appearing, tiny at first, then larger, growing ever bigger, and in his mind it took on the aspect of a tramp-steamer, as if he was about to set off on a long voyage, across the seas, to see new people and unknown things. It came alongside and he got a ticket. People in their Sunday best were already aboard, wearing showy outfits with gaudy ribbons on their hats and with fat scarlet faces. Patissot found a place right in the bow, standing up, legs apart like a sailor, to make himself look well travelled. But since he was worried about the slight wash of the boat he braced himself on his walking stick, the better to keep his balance.

After the stop at the Point-du-Jour the river began to widen, peaceful in the brilliant light; then, when they had passed between two islands, the boat followed the curve of a hillside whose greenery was covered with white houses. A voice announced Bas-Meudon, then Sèvres, at last Saint-Cloud, and Patissot got off.

Once on the quay he opened his ordnance survey map, so as not to make any mistakes.

In any case, it was quite clear. He would go by that path to find La Celle, turn left, go a little obliquely to the right, and by that road he would reach Versailles, where he would visit the park before having dinner.

The path was climbing and Patissot was puffing, crushed under his bag, his legs uncomfortable in his gaiters, and dragging his big shoes in the dust, heavier than a ball and chain. All at once he stopped with a gesture of despair. In the haste of his departure he had forgotten the marine telescope!

At last, here were the woods. Then despite the frightful heat, despite the sweat running down his forehead, the weight of his trappings and the lurches of his bag, he ran, or rather trotted towards the verdure with little jumps, as old, broken-winded horses do.

He went into the shade, into delicious coolness, and felt overcome by emotion at the multitudes of different little flowers spread all along the ditches, yellow, red, blue, violet, charming, delicate, long-stemmed. Insects of all colours and shapes, squat, elongated, extraordinarily constructed, frightening and microscopic monsters, were painfully climbing up blades of grass which bent under their weight. And Patissot sincerely admired creation. But, since he was exhausted, he sat down.

Then he felt like eating. He was horrified, however, at the inside of his bag. One of the bottles had broken, undoubtedly when he had fallen, and the liquid, contained by the waterproof oilcloth, had made a wine soup from his numerous provisions. All the same he ate a slice of carefully wiped leg of lamb, a piece of ham and some soggy red crusts of bread, quenching his thirst with some fermented Bordeaux covered with an unsightly pink scum.

And when he had rested a few hours, after having once more consulted his map, he set off again.

After a while he found himself at a crossroads which nothing had led him to expect. He looked at the sun, tried to orientate himself, reflected, studied at length all the little criss-crossing lines on the paper that signified routes, and soon became convinced that he was completely lost.

Before him an entrancing avenue opened up, its rather thin foliage letting drops of sunlight rain down everywhere on the ground, lighting up white marguerites hidden in the grass. It went on interminably, empty and calm. Only a big hornet, solitary and buzzing, was following it, stopping sometimes on a flower which would nod under its weight, and going off almost at once to land again a little further off. Its enormous body seemed like brown velvet striped with yellow, carried on wings which were transparent and incredibly small. Patissot was watching it with deep interest, when something moved under his feet. At first it frightened him, and he jumped aside; then, leaning over carefully, he spied a frog, as big as a hazelnut, which was making huge leaps.

He bent to pick it up, but it slipped through his hands. Then, with infinite care, he crawled towards it on his knees, advancing very gently, the bag on his back looking like a huge shell and giving him the appearance of a big tortoise as he moved along. When he was close to the spot where the creature had stopped he took action, flung his two hands forward, fell on his nose in the grass, and came up with two fistfuls of earth but no frog. He looked in vain, and did not find it again.

As soon as he had got himself on his feet he noticed two people far in the distance who were coming towards him making gestures. A woman was waving a parasol, and a man, in shirt sleeves, was carrying his coat over his arm. Then the woman began to run, calling, 'Monsieur, monsieur!'

He wiped his forehead and replied, 'Madame!'

'Monsieur, we are lost, completely lost!'

Reticence prevented him from making the same admission and he pronounced gravely, 'You are on the Versailles road.'

'What, on the Versailles road? But we are going to Rueil.'

He was perturbed, but nevertheless replied boldly, 'Madame, I will show you on my ordnance survey map that you really are on the Versailles road.'

The husband was coming up. He had a bewildered, despairing look. The woman, young, pretty, an energetic brunette, flew into a temper as soon as he came close to her: 'Just look what you've done! We are at Versailles now. Come on, look at the ordnance survey map the gentleman is so kind as to show you — that is, if you know how to read it! My God! My God! How stupid some people are! I told you to go to the right, but you wouldn't; you always think you know everything.'

The poor young man seemed disconsolate. He replied, 'But my love, it's you …' She did not let him finish, and blamed him for her whole life, from the time of their marriage right up to the present moment. He was turning sorrowful eyes towards the undergrowth, seeming to want to penetrate its depths, and from time to time, as though overtaken by madness, he would utter a piercing cry, something like 'tiiit', which did not at all seem to surprise his wife but which completely astonished Patissot.

The young woman suddenly turned to the clerk with a smile: 'If monsieur will permit it, we will go along with him so that we don't get lost again and risk sleeping in the woods.' Unable to refuse, he agreed, his heart tortured with anxiety, not knowing where he was going to take them.

They walked for a long time, the man still crying 'tiiit'; night fell. The veil of mist which covers the countryside at dusk was slowly spreading, and a sort of poetry was floating, made up of that special and charming feeling of coolness that fills the woods at the approach of night. The little woman had taken Patissot's arm and was continuing, through her rosy mouth, to spit complaints at her husband who, without answering her, was incessantly shouting 'tiiit' more and more loudly.

The big clerk finally asked him, 'Why are you shouting like that?'

The other, with tears in his eyes, answered him, 'It's my poor dog that I've lost.'

'What! You have lost your dog?'

'Yes, we brought him up in Paris; he had never been to the country, and when he saw the leaves he was so happy that he began to run as if he was mad. He went into the woods, and for all I've called him he has not come back. He is going to die of hunger in there … tiiit …'

The woman shrugged her shoulders: 'When you are as stupid as you, you don't keep a dog!' But he stopped, feeling his body feverishly. She watched him: 'Well, what?'

'I hadn't noticed that I had my coat over my arm … I have lost my wallet … My money was in it.'

This time she choked with rage: 'Well, go and look for it!'

He answered her gently, 'Yes, my love; where shall I find you again?'

Patissot replied daringly, 'But at Versailles!' And having heard mention of the Hotel des Reservoirs, he named it.

The husband turned round and, bent towards the ground which he was anxiously searching with his eyes, constantly crying 'tiiit', he moved off. He took a long time to disappear; the thickening shadows closed around him, and still his voice, from far away, was sending back its pitiful 'tiiit', becoming more piercing as the night grew blacker and his hope faded.

Patissot was delightfully moved when he found himself alone, in the bushy shade of the woods, at this languorous hour of dusk, with this pretty unknown woman who was leaning on his arm. And, for the first time in his egotistical life, he felt the charm of poetic love, the pleasure of abandon and the enveloping complicity of nature in our feelings. He was searching for gallant words, which he did not find, however. But a main road came into view and houses appeared to the right; a man passed by. Patissot, trembling, asked where they were.

'Bougival.'

'What! Bougival? Are you sure?'

'Yes, indeed I am!'

The woman laughed like a little madwoman – the idea of her lost husband made her sick with joy. They had dinner at the water's edge, in a countryside restaurant. She was charming, vivacious, telling hundreds of amusing stories, which were slightly turning the head of her neighbour. Then, on leaving, she cried, 'I've just thought, I haven't a sou, as my husband lost his wallet.' Patissot hastened to open his purse and offered to lend her what she needed; he took out a louis, feeling that he couldn't give her less. She said nothing, but held out her hand, took the money, said a grave 'thank you' soon followed by a smile, simperingly adjusted her hat before the mirror, did not let him accompany her, now that she knew where to go, and finally left like a bird flying away, while Patissot, very gloomy, made a mental reckoning of the day's expenses.

He didn't go to the Ministry the next day, he had such a terrible migraine.

III
At a friend's house

Throughout the week Patissot told of his adventure, and he described poetically the places he had gone to, feeling indignant when he found so little enthusiasm around him. Only an old, invariably taciturn dispatch clerk, Monsieur Boivin, nicknamed Boileau,*

---

* Comic effect: Nicholas Boileau (1636–1711), critic, poet, satirist, noted for his sense of form and style.

gave him consistent attention. He lived in the country himself, he had a little garden which he cultivated carefully, was content with little and was perfectly happy, so it was said. Patissot could now understand his tastes, and the similarity of their aspirations made them friends at once. To cement this budding sympathy, old man Boivin invited him to lunch at his little house in Colombes the following Sunday.

Patissot took the eight o'clock train and after a great deal of searching he found, right in the middle of the town, a kind of obscure alley, a filthy cesspool between two high walls and, right at the end, a rotting door closed with string wound round two nails. He opened it and found himself face to face with an indescribable creature who must nevertheless have been a woman. Her chest seemed to be wrapped in dirty cloths, ragged petticoats were hanging round her hips and pigeon feathers were fluttering in her tangled hair. She was looking furiously at the visitor with her little grey eyes; then, after a moment's silence, she asked, 'What do you want?'

'Monsieur Boivin.'

'This is it. What do you want Monsieur Boivin for?'

'He is expecting me.'

She looked even fiercer and went on, 'Ah! Is it you who's coming to lunch?'

He stammered a trembling 'Yes'. Then, turning towards the house, she shouted in an angry voice, 'Boivin, your man's here.'

Little old Boivin at once appeared on the doorstep of a sort of plastered hut, roofed with zinc, with only a ground floor, and which looked like a footwarmer.* He was wearing white drill

---

* Maupassant means a kind of metal box with holes in the lid, to take hot coals.

trousers spattered with coffee stains and a dirty panama. After shaking hands with Patissot he led him into what he called his garden: at the end of another filthy passageway, it was a little square of ground as big as a handkerchief surrounded with houses so high that it was only in the sun for two or three hours a day. Pansies, carnations, wallflowers, a few rose bushes were in their death throes at the bottom of this airless pit, heated like an oven by the reflected heat of the roofs.

'I have no trees,' said Boivin, 'but the neighbours' walls do me instead, and I have shade like in a wood.'

Then, holding Patissot by a button: 'You can do me a favour. You saw the wife; she's not amenable, is she? But that's not all, wait until lunch. Imagine! To stop me going out she won't give me my office clothes and only leaves me with old things too worn out for town. Today I've got clean ones; I told her we would have dinner together. That's arranged. But I can't do the watering for fear of soiling my trousers. If I soil my trousers I'm done for! I'm counting on you, is that all right?'

Agreeing to do it, Patissot took off his frock-coat, rolled up his sleeves and set to work with all his might at a sort of pump which whistled, puffed and croaked like a consumptive, only to let out a thin trickle of water like the flow of a Wallace drinking fountain.[*] It took ten minutes to fill a watering can. Patissot was dripping. Old Boivin directed him: 'Here, on this plant ... a bit more ... That's enough! Now this one.'

But the watering can had a hole in it and was leaking, and Patissot's feet were getting more water than the flowers; the bottoms of his trousers, soaking, were getting covered in mud. Twenty

---

[*] Some are still to be seen in Paris streets, named after Sir Richard Wallace, their provider.

times over he began again, soaking his feet again, sweating again as he made the pump wheel squeak; and when he wanted to stop, worn out, old Boivin pleadingly tugged at his arm.

'One more watering can, just one, and it'll be done.'

To thank him he presented him with a rose, but this rose had opened so fully that on contact with Patissot's coat every one of its petals fell out, leaving a sort of greenish pear in his buttonhole which very much took him aback. He did not dare to say anything, being circumspect. Boivin pretended not to see.

Then the distant voice of Madame Boivin was heard: 'Well, are you coming then? You've been told it's ready!'

They went towards the footwarmer, quaking like two guilty men.

If the garden was in the shade, the house, on the other hand, was in full sun, and the heat of no oven could match its interior.

Three plates, flanked by badly washed tin cutlery, were sticking to the ancient grease of a pine table, in the middle of which was an earthenware bowl containing threads of old reheated boiled meat in some sort of liquid, in which were swimming some spotty potatoes. They sat down. They ate.

A big carafe full of water faintly coloured red caught Patissot's eye. A little embarrassed, Boivin said to his wife, 'Look here, my dear, just this once won't you give us a little pure wine?'

She stared at him furiously: 'So you two can get drunk, is that it, and hang around my house shouting all day? Thanks for the suggestion!'

They kept quiet. After the stew, she brought in another course of potatoes done with a bit of utterly rancid bacon; when this new dish was finished, still in silence, she declared, 'That's it. Now be off with you.'

Boivin looked at her, astounded. 'What about the pigeon? The pigeon you were plucking this morning?'

She put her hands on her hips. 'Haven't you had enough, then? Just because you bring people here that's no reason to devour everything in the house. What am I supposed to eat this evening, monsieur?'

The two men got up, went just outside the door, and little old man Boivin, known as Boileau, whispered in Patissot's ear: 'Wait for me a minute and we'll be off!'

He went into the other room to get ready, and Patissot over-heard this dialogue:

'Will you give me twenty sous, my dear?'

'What do you want with twenty sous?'

'You never know what might happen; it's always a good idea to have some money on you.'

She shouted, so she could be heard outside, 'No, monsieur, I won't give it you; since this man has taken lunch at your house, the least he can do is pay your expenses for the day.'

Old Boivin came back to fetch Patissot, but the latter, wanting to be polite, bowed to the mistress of the house and stammered, 'Madame … my thanks …gracious welcome …'

She replied, 'All right. But don't you go bringing him back drunk, because you'll have me to reckon with, you know!'

They left.

They reached the banks of the Seine, opposite an island planted with poplars. Boivin, looking lovingly at the river, squeezed his neighbour's arm: 'Ah! In a week we'll be there, Monsieur Patissot.'

'Where will we be, Monsieur Boivin?'

'Why, fishing; the season opens on the fifteenth.'

Patissot felt a slight tremble, like a first meeting with the woman who will ravage your soul. He replied, 'Oh! So you're an angler, Monsieur Boivin?'

'Am I an angler, monsieur! Fishing is my passion!'

Patissot questioned him with deep interest. Boivin told him the names of all the fish that frolicked beneath the black water before them ... and Patissot believed he was seeing them. Boivin listed the hooks, the bait, the places, the right times for each species ... and Patissot felt he was becoming more of a fisherman than Boivin himself. They agreed that the following Sunday they would open the season together, for Patissot's instruction, and the latter congratulated himself on finding so experienced an initiator.

They stopped for dinner at a sort of obscure den used by bargees and all the local riff-raff. At the door old Boivin took the precaution of saying, 'It doesn't look up to much, but you do very well here.'

They sat at a table. By the second glass of Argenteuil Patissot understood why Madame Boivin only served her husband Abondance* – the drink was going to the little fellow's head. He was declaiming, he got to his feet, he wanted to demonstrate his strength, he tried to break up a fight between two quarrelling drunks and would have been knocked out along with Patissot if the landlord had not intervened. By the coffee stage he was so intoxicated, despite his friend's efforts to stop him drinking, that he could not walk, and when they left Patissot was holding him up by the arms.

They plunged into the darkness across the plain, lost their way and wandered about for a long time; then all at once they found themselves in the middle of a forest of posts which came up to eye level. It was a vine with its stakes. For a long while they kept moving through it, hesitating, panic-stricken, retracing their steps

---

* Argenteuil is poor-quality local wine; Abondance is wine diluted with a good quantity of water.

without being able to find the way out. Finally little old Boivin, known as Boileau, fell over a stick which lacerated his face; otherwise unperturbed, he remained seated on the ground and, with drunken obstinacy, vociferously emitted long and resounding 'tum-te-tums', while a bewildered Patissot called to the four points of the compass: 'Hello, anybody! Hello, anybody!'

A farm worker out late rescued them and put them back on their path.

Getting near the Boivins' house was terrifying Patissot. At last they reached the door, which suddenly opened before them and Madame Boivin appeared like an ancient Fury, a candle in her hand. As soon as she saw her husband she rushed at Patissot crying, 'Oh! You scoundrel! I just knew you'd get him drunk.'

The poor fellow was frightened silly, let go of his friend, who collapsed into the greasy mud of the alley, and fled as fast as his legs would carry him until he reached the railway station.

IV
Angling

The evening before the day when, for the first time in his life, he would have to cast a hook into a river, Monsieur Patissot acquired for the sum of eighty centimes *The Perfect Angler*. He learned a thousand useful things from this work, but he was particularly struck by the style, and he remembered the following passage:

> In a word, with no effort, with no documentation, with no guidance, would you like to achieve results and fish successfully to the right, to the left or in front of you, downstream or upstream, with an air of victory which allows of no difficulty? Well, go fishing before, during and after a storm, when the heavens open and are zigzagged with lines of fire, when the

earth is moved by the prolonged rumblings of thunder; then, whether from greed or terror, the usual habits of all the agitated, turbulent fish become confused into a kind of universal gallop.

In this confusion, whether you follow or ignore all the diagnostics of favourable opportunities, go fishing and you will march to victory!

Then, so as to be able to catch fishes of different sizes at the same time, he bought three superior pieces of equipment, rods for in town, lines for the river, which unreeled endlessly with just a jerk. For gudgeon he had No. 15 hooks, for bream No. 12s, and with the No. 7s he was very much counting on filling his basket with carp and barbel. He did not buy mud-worms, which he was sure to find everywhere, but he acquired a supply of maggots. He had a big pot of them, quite full, and in the evening he took a look at them. The hideous creatures, giving off an unspeakable stench, were wriggling in their bath of bran as they do in rotting meat; and Patissot wanted to practise hanging them on the hooks. With repugnance he took hold of one of them, but scarcely had he put it on the sharp point of the curved steel when it burst and completely collapsed. He began again twenty times in succession without any better success, and he might have gone on all night if he had not been afraid of exhausting his entire supply of vermin.

He left by the first train. The station was full of people armed with fishing rods. Some, like Patissot's, appeared to be simple bamboos; but others, in a single piece, tapered as they rose into the air. It was like a forest of thin sticks that were constantly bumping into each other, mingling, seeming to be fighting each other like rapiers or swaying like masts above an ocean of wide-brimmed straw hats.

When the engine moved off you could see them poking out of all the doors, and as the upper deck was bristling with them from one end of the convoy to the other, the train had the appearance of a long caterpillar winding across the plain.

They got out at Courbevoie, and the Bezons coach was taken by storm. A heap of fishermen were squashed together on the roof and, since they were holding their rods in their hands, the old bone-shaker suddenly took on the aspect of a large porcupine.

All along the road you could see men heading in the same direction, as though on a huge pilgrimage to some unknown Jerusalem. They were carrying their long pointed sticks, reminiscent of the quarterstaffs shouldered by the ancient believers as they returned from Palestine, and their tin boxes were bouncing on their backs. They were in a hurry.

At Bezons the river appeared. On each bank was a line of people, some men in coats, others in drill, others in overalls; women, even children and marriageable young girls, were fishing.

Patissot made for the weir, where his friend Boivin was awaiting him. The latter's welcome was chilly. He had just made the acquaintance of a big man of about fifty, who appeared to be very knowledgeable, with a face burnt by the sun. The three of them hired a big boat and planned to tie up almost under the fall of the weir, in the disturbed water where you get the most fish.

Boivin was ready at once. Having baited his line he cast it, then remained motionless, fixing his eyes on the little float with extraordinary concentration. But from time to time he would pull his line out of the water and cast it a little further off. The big man, when he had sent well-baited hooks into the river, placed his line at his side, filled his pipe, lit it, crossed his arms and, without a glance at the float, watched the flow of the water. Patissot once more began to burst his maggots. After five minutes he appealed to Boivin, 'Monsieur Boivin, would you be so kind as to put these creatures on my hook. I've tried in vain, I can't do it.' Boivin lifted his head. 'Please don't disturb me, Monsieur Patissot; we are not here for fun.' All the same he baited the line, which Patissot cast, carefully imitating all his friend's movements.

The boat was dancing crazily next to the falling water; the waves were tossing it, sudden turns in the current were making it wheel like a top, even though it was moored by both ends, and Patissot, completely absorbed in fishing, was feeling a vague unease, a heaviness in his head, a strange giddiness.

However, they were not catching anything. Little old man Boivin was looking very nervous, making curt gestures and desperate shakes of the head; Patissot was as distressed as though it was a disaster; only the big man, still motionless, was quietly smoking, without bothering about his line. In the end Patissot, in despair, turned to him and said in a sad voice: 'They are not biting?'

The other simply replied, 'Evidently not!'

Patissot, astonished, looked at him. 'Do you sometimes catch a lot?'

'Never!'

'What do you mean, never?'

The big man, still smoking like a factory chimney, let slip these words which upset his neighbour's thinking: 'It would seriously inconvenience me if they did bite. I don't come to fish, me, I come because it's very comfortable here: the motion is like being at sea; I only bring a line because everyone else does.'

Monsieur Patissot, on the other hand, was no longer at all comfortable. His unease, vague at first, was still increasing and finally took form. They were indeed shaken like at sea, and he was suffering from seasickness.

After the first attack had calmed down a little, he suggested he should leave, but Boivin was furious and nearly flew at him. However, moved by pity, the big man firmly decided to bring in the boat and, when Patissot's giddiness had subsided, they turned their attention to lunch.

Two restaurants were possible.

One very small one, which had the look of a *guinguette*,* was frequented by the small fry among the anglers. The other, bearing the name Lime Tree Chalet, looked like a middle-class villa and took as its customers the aristocracy of the rod. The two land-lords, enemies from birth, glared at each other across the big plot of ground that separated them; here stood the white house inhabited by the fishing warden and the weir-keeper. Now one of these authorities gave his allegiance to the *guinguette* and the other to 'The Lime Tree', so that the inner differences of opinion of these three isolated houses reproduced the history of all humanity.

Boivin, who knew the *guinguette*, wanted to go there: 'They serve you very well there and it's not expensive. You'll see. And by the way, Monsieur Patissot, don't expect to get me tipsy as you did last Sunday. My wife was furious, you know, and she swore she would never forgive you!'

The big man declared he would only eat at 'The Lime Tree', because it was, he affirmed, an excellent establishment where the cooking matched the best restaurants in Paris. 'Do as you like,' declared Boivin, 'I'm going where I usually go.' And he went. Patissot, displeased with his friend, followed the big man.

The two had lunch together, exchanged views, shared impressions and realized they were destined to get along.

After the meal everyone went back to fishing, but the two new

---

* An open-air café and bar with music and dancing, usually in the country.

friends went off together along the bank, stopped by the railway bridge and cast their lines into the water as they chatted. Still nothing was biting; Patissot had now come to terms with this.

A family approached them. The father, sporting a lawyer's side-whiskers, was holding a rod of inordinate length; three children of the male sex, of different sizes, were carrying bamboos of varying dimensions according to age, and the mother, who was very stout, was gracefully handling a charming fishing rod decorated with a ribbon on the handle. The father greeted them with: 'Is this a good spot, gentlemen?' Patissot was about to speak, when his neighbour replied 'Excellent!' The whole family smiled and settled down around the two anglers. Now Patissot was seized with a wild desire to catch a fish, just one, no matter what, the size of a fly, to win the respect of all these people, and he began to manoeuvre his line as he had seen Boivin do during the morning. He let the float follow the current until the line was played out, giving it a jerk, pulling the hooks out of the river, then, making them describe a large circle in the air, he cast them back into the water a few metres higher up. He was beginning to think he had got the hang of carrying out this movement elegantly when his line, which he had just pulled out with a quick flick of the wrist, got caught somewhere behind him. He pulled hard; there was a loud cry to the rear and he observed, describing a meteoric curve in the sky and fastened on to one of his hooks, a magnificent feminine hat laden with flowers, which he deposited, still on the end of his line, right in the middle of the river.

He turned round in dismay, letting go of his rod, which followed the hat, slipping away with the current, while the big man, his new friend, lay flat on his back roaring with laughter. The lady, hatless and astounded, was speechless with rage; her husband was thoroughly angry and demanded the price of the hat, which

Patissot paid at three times its worth.

Then the family made a dignified departure.

Patissot took another rod and bathed his maggots until evening. His neighbour slept tranquilly on the grass. He woke up around seven o'clock.

'Let's go,' he said.

Patissot pulled in his line, cried out and fell on his behind with astonishment. A little fish was swinging on the end of the line. Closer inspection revealed that it was hooked by the middle of its belly; a hook had snagged it in passing as it came out of the water.

It was a triumph – immoderate joy. Patissot wanted to have it fried just for him.

During dinner his intimacy with his new acquaintance increased. He learned that this individual was living in Argenteuil and had sailed for thirty years without being put off it; he agreed to have lunch at his place the following Sunday, with the promise of a good sailing trip in the *Diver*, his friend's clipper.

The conversation interested him so much that he forgot his catch.

The thought only occurred to him after coffee, and he insisted it was brought to him. It was like a sort of twisted and yellowish matchstick in the middle of the plate. All the same he ate it with pride and, on the bus in the evening, he told his neighbours that during the day he had caught fourteen pounds of little fish for frying.

V
Two famous men

Monsieur Patissot had promised his sailing friend that he would spend the following Sunday with him. Something unexpected upset his plans. One evening on the Boulevard he met one of his cousins, whom he very rarely saw. He was a likeable journalist, very involved in every kind of society, and he offered to show Patissot a number of interesting things.

'What are you doing on Sunday, for instance?'

'I'm going to Argenteuil, sailing.'

'Come on, sailing's boring; it's always the same. Look, I'll take you with me. I'll introduce you to two famous men and we will see the houses of two artists.'

'But I've been told to go to the country!'

'We are going to the country. On the way I'm going to pay a visit to Meissonier at his house in Poissy; then we will walk as far as Médan, where Zola lives, as I need to ask if our paper can serialize his next novel.'*

Patissot agreed, beside himself with joy.

He even bought a new frock coat, as his old one was a little worn and he wanted to appear presentable. Like everyone who talks about arts that they have never practised, he was horribly afraid of saying something foolish, either to the artist or to the man of letters. He conveyed his fears to his cousin, who began to laugh as he answered, 'Nonsense! Just pay them compliments, nothing but compliments, and more compliments; that makes the foolish things go down better if you do say any. Do you know Meissonier's pictures?'

'Very well, I believe.'

'Have you read the Rougon-Macquart books?'

'From end to end.'

---

* Maupassant knew Zola well and may have known Meissonier (1815–91) too. The details of Zola's house, which can still be visited, are all quite correct, but in 1880 Zola had not yet built the second large tower.

'That's enough. Name a picture from time to time, refer to a novel here and there, and add: Superb!!! Extraordinary!!! Wonderful execution!!! Curiously powerful, etc. You can always get by like that. Of course those two are awfully blasé about everything, but you know praise always pleases an artist.'

On Sunday morning they left for Poissy.

A few steps from the station, at the end of the church square, they found Meissonier's house. After passing under a low red-painted doorway which opened on to a magnificent vine arbour, the journalist stopped and, turning towards his companion, asked: 'How do you picture Meissonier?'

Patissot hesitated. At last he made up his mind: 'A small man, very neat, clean shaven, military air.' The other smiled. 'Very well. Come along.' A building in the form of a country cottage, very bizarre, appeared on the left, and to the right, almost opposite and a little lower down, was the main house. It was an unusual construction in which there was a little of everything – gothic fortress, manor house, villa, thatched cottage, mansion, cathedral, mosque, pyramid, *gâteau de Savoie*,* something oriental and something occidental. A superlatively complicated style, enough to drive a classical architect insane, and yet it had something pretty and fantastic, invented by the artist himself and built under his supervision.

They entered. A number of trunks were cluttering up a little parlour. A man appeared, small and wearing a sailor's jersey, but what was striking about him was his beard – the beard of a prophet, incredible, a river, a streaming flow, a Niagara of a beard. He greeted the journalist: 'Excuse me, my dear sir; I only arrived yesterday and everything is still upside down here. Do sit down.' The other declined, excusing himself: 'My dear master, I just

---

* Very light sponge cake made in an ornamental fluted mould.

dropped by to pay my compliments.' Patissot, who felt very uneasy, bowed at each of his friend's words, as though by some automatic motion, and murmured, stammering a little, 'What a su-su-superb property!' The artist, flattered, smiled and suggested they look around.

First he took them into a little house with a medieval appearance which was his former studio, opening on to a *terrace*. Then they went through a sitting room, a dining room, a hall full of marvellous works of art, delightful tapestries from Beauvais, the Gobelins and Flanders. But the bizarrely ornamental profusion of the outside became a prodigious profusion of staircases on the inside. A magnificent main staircase, a hidden staircase in a tower, service stairs in another, stairs everywhere! Patissot, by chance, opened a door and fell back in amazement. There was a *temple*, that place whose name respectable people pronounce only in English, an original and charming sanctuary in exquisite taste, ornamented like a pagoda and obviously decorated with a great deal of thought.

They visited the park, which was complex, undulating, tortuous, full of old trees. But the journalist was determined to leave and, with many thanks, took leave of the master. As they went out they met a gardener. Patissot asked him, 'Has Monsieur Meissonier owned this place for a long time?' The good fellow answered, 'Oh, monsieur, I'll have to explain. He bought the land in 1846, but the house! He has already demolished and rebuilt it five or six times since then ... I'm sure he's put two million into it, monsieur!'

And Patissot, as he went on his way, was filled with immense respect for this man, not so much because of his great success, his fame and his talent, but because he spent so much money on a fantasy, while the ordinary bourgeois deprives himself of all fantasy to amass money!

After they had passed through Poissy they went on foot along the road to Médan. At first the road follows the Seine, with many lovely islands at that point, then it climbs up to the pretty village of Villennes, descends a little and finally reaches the area inhabited by the author of the Rougon-Macquart books.

A pretty old church, flanked by two small towers, was the first thing to appear on the left. They went on a few paces, and a passing farmer showed them the novelist's door.

Before going in they looked at the building. A big, new, square construction, very tall, seemed to have given birth, like the mountain in the fable, to a very small white house, which crouched at its feet. This house, the original dwelling, had been built by the former owner. The tower was built by Zola.

They rang the bell. An enormous dog, a cross between a mountain dog and a Newfoundland, began to howl so dreadfully that Patissot felt a vague wish to retrace his steps. But a servant ran up and calmed Bertrand, opened the door and took the journalist's card to give to his master.

'Let's hope he'll see us!' murmured Patissot. 'It would be terribly tedious to have come this far without seeing him.'

His companion smiled: 'Never fear, I have an idea how to get in.'

But the servant returned and simply asked them to follow him.

They went into the new building. Patissot, very excited, started to puff as he climbed an old-style staircase which led them to the second floor.

As he did so he tried to imagine this man whose sonorous and glorious name was reverberating at this moment at all the ends of the earth, amid furious hatred from some people, real or simulated indignation from high society, envious disdain from some of his colleagues, the respect of a horde of readers and the frenzied admiration of many. He expected to see a sort of bearded giant, fearful in aspect, with a booming voice, and at first not very pleasing.

The door opened on to an inordinately large, tall room, lit from side to side by a single window which looked out over the open country. Old tapestries covered the walls, and to the left there was a monumental fireplace, flanked by two stone men, that could have burned a hundred-year-old oak tree in a day. An immense table, laden with papers, books and newspapers, occupied the centre of this living space. It was so vast and grandiose that it monopolized the eye at first, and only afterwards was the attention drawn to a man, who as they entered was stretched out on an oriental divan on which twenty people could have slept.

He took a few steps towards them, greeted them, indicated two chairs with his hand and went back to his divan, tucking one leg under him. A book was lying by his side, and with his right hand he was playing with an ivory paper knife, whose point he contemplated at intervals with only one eye, shutting the other with the persistence of the short-sighted.

While the journalist was explaining the reason for his visit, and the writer looked at him fixedly from time to time, listening without yet replying, Patissot, who felt more and more embarrassed, contemplated this celebrity.

Aged scarcely forty, he was of average height, quite fat and good-natured in appearance. His head (very like those found in many Italian paintings of the sixteenth century), without being beautiful in the plastic sense of the word, bore the firm stamp of intelligence and power. His short hair stood up on his very prominent forehead. A straight nose stopped, cut short, as though by too brusque a use of scissors, above his upper lip, which was darkened by a quite thick black moustache, and his whole chin was covered with a very close-clipped beard. His dark gaze, often ironic, was penetrating; you could feel that behind it there was an always active mind working away, piercing people, interpreting words, analysing gestures, laying the heart bare. This round and strong head certainly went with his name, short and quick, with its two syllables leaping to the sound of two vowels.

When the journalist had finished his sales talk, the writer answered that he did not want to commit himself, he would see later on, even the outline was not finished yet. Then he fell silent. It was a dismissal, and the two men, a little embarrassed, got up. But a desire came over Patissot: he wanted this famous character to say something to him, any old thing, which he could repeat to his colleagues, and, growing daring, he stammered, 'Oh, monsieur, if you knew how I appreciate your books!' The other man bowed, but did not reply. Patissot became bold and went on, 'It is a great honour for me to speak to you today.' The writer bowed again, but with a stiff and impatient air. Patissot noticed it and, losing his head, he added as he was leaving, 'What a su-su-superb property!'

Then awoke in the indifferent heart of the man of letters the property owner and, smiling, he opened the windows to show the extent of the view. A colossal skyline spread out in every direction; there was Triel, Pisse-Fontaine, Chanteloup, all the heights of Hautrie and the Seine, as far as the eye could see. The two visitors were in ecstasy and congratulated him, and the house was laid open to them. They saw everything, down to the elegant kitchen whose walls and even the ceiling, covered in blue and white tiles, excited the astonishment of the countryfolk.

'How did you come to buy this house?' asked the journalist. The novelist recounted how, looking for a cottage to rent one summer, he had found the little house, now joined to the new one, on sale for a few thousand francs, a trifle, almost nothing. He bought it on the spot.

'But everything you have added to it must have cost a lot afterwards?'

The writer smiled, 'Yes, quite a bit!'

And the two men left.

The journalist, holding Patissot by the arm, was philosophizing, talking slowly: 'Every general has his Waterloo,' he said, 'every Balzac has his Jardies,* and every artist who lives in the country has his pride of ownership.'

They took the train at the station in Villennes, and in the carriage Patissot loudly dropped the names of the famous painter and the great novelist, as though they were his friends. He was trying to give the impression that he had had lunch at the house of one and dinner with the other.

VI
Before the public holiday

The public holiday is getting closer, and already agitation is running through the streets like the surface of the waves when a storm is coming.† The shops, decorated with flags, are hanging all the gaiety of a dyeworks at their doors, and the haberdashers are stocking up on the three colours just as grocers do with candles. Little by little spirits are rising; people are talking about it after dinner on the pavements; they have thoughts to share:

'What a holiday it's going to be, my friends, what a holiday!'

'Didn't you know? All the royalty are coming to see it incognito, as private people.'

---

* The name of Balzac's house at Sèvres.

† The fourteenth of July, Bastille Day, became a public holiday for the first time in 1880; this story appeared only a few days before.

'Apparently the Emperor of Russia has arrived; he is planning to walk about everywhere with the Prince of Wales.'

'Oh, as holidays go, it's going to be quite a holiday!'

It will be a holiday; what Monsieur Patissot, Parisian bourgeois, calls a holiday – one of those unspeakable throngs which for fifteen hours rolls out from one end of the city to the other every physical ugliness decked in tawdry finery, a swell of sweating bodies, tossing together the bulky busybody in tricolour ribbons, grown fat behind her counter and complaining of shortness of breath, with the under nourished office worker dragging along his wife and his little one, the workman carrying his astride his shoulders, the bewildered provincial looking like a stunned cretin, the half-shaven groom still smelling of the stable. Then there are the foreigners like dressed-up monkeys, Englishwomen like giraffes, the well-scrubbed water carrier and the uncountable host of the lower middle classes, harmless people of independent means who are amused by everything. O bustle, exhaustion, sweat and dust, shouting, heave of human flesh, crushed corns, confusion of all thought, frightful smells, pointless movement, the breath of multitudes, garlic-laden air – give Monsieur Patissot all the joy his heart could wish!

He made his plans after having read the Mayor's proclamation posted on the walls in his district.

This prose declared: 'I am calling your attention in particular to the private celebrations. Decorate your houses, light up your windows. Get together, subscribe together to give your houses, your street a brighter, more artistic appearance than the houses in the neighbouring streets.'

So Monsieur Patissot laboriously searched for some artistic appearance that he could give his lodgings.

There was a serious problem. His only window gave on to a

yard, a dark, narrow, well-like yard where only the rats would be able to see his three Chinese lanterns.

He needed an opening on to the public way. He found it. A rich man of private means, noble and royalist, lived on the first floor of his house, and his coachman, who was also a reactionary, occupied an attic room that gave on to the street. Monsieur Patissot assumed that every conscience had its price, so he offered a hundred sous to this citizen of the whip to let him have his lodging from midday to midnight. The offer was accepted at once.

Then he worried about the decorations.

Three flags, four lanterns, was that enough to give this attic window an artistic appearance? To express all the elevated emotion of his soul? No, certainly not! But in spite of lengthy research and nightly meditation, Monsieur Patissot could not come up with anything else. He consulted his neighbours, who were surprised by his questions; he interrogated his colleagues. Everyone had bought lanterns and flags, adding tricolour decorations to them for the daytime.

So he applied himself to finding an original idea. He went to cafés and approached the customers; they were lacking in imagination. Then one morning he went on the top of an omnibus. A gentleman with a respectable air was smoking a cigar beside him; a workman, further off, was smoking his upside-down pipe; two layabouts were cracking jokes near the coachman; and white-collar workers of all kinds were going to their jobs on a three-sou ticket.

On the shop fronts bunches of flags were resplendent in the morning sun. Patissot turned to his neighbour.

'It will be a lovely holiday,' he said.

The gentleman looked at him askance and announced with an arrogant air, 'It's all the same to me.'

'Aren't you going to join in?' asked the stunned office worker.

The other shook his head in disdain and declared, 'I feel sorry for them with their holiday. What's the holiday for? Is it from the government? As for myself, I don't recognize the government, monsieur!'

But Patissot, who was a government employee himself, got on his high horse and said in a firm voice, 'The government, monsieur, is the Republic.'

His neighbour was not put down and, tranquilly putting his hands in his pockets, replied: 'So? I'm not against it. The Republic or anything else, it's all the same to me. What I want, monsieur, is to get to know my government. I saw Charles X, and I supported him, monsieur; I saw Louis-Philippe, and I supported him, monsieur; I saw Napoléon, and I supported him; but I have never seen the Republic.'

Patissot, still serious, replied, 'It is represented by its President.'

The other grunted, 'Well, let them show him to me.'

Patissot shrugged his shoulders. 'Everyone can see him; he is not in a cupboard.'

But all of a sudden the big man got carried away. 'Excuse me, monsieur, you can't see him. I myself have tried more than a hundred times. I lay in wait near the Elysée; he didn't come out. A passer-by assured me he was playing billiards in the café opposite; he was not there. They promised me he would go to Melun for the agricultural show; I went to Melun and I didn't see him. I got tired of it in the end. I didn't see Monsieur Gambetta either, and I don't even know a Deputy.'

He was getting worked up. 'A government should show itself, monsieur; that's what it's for, not for anything else. You should know that on a certain day, at a certain time, the government will pass by in a certain street. That way you go and you're satisfied.'

Patissot, calmed down, considered these reasons. 'It is true,' he said, 'that people like to be familiar with who's governing them.'

The man adopted a gentler tone: 'Do you know how I myself would want to see the holiday? Well, monsieur, I would have a procession of golden chariots, like the carriages for the King's coronation; and in them I would show off the members of the government around Paris for the whole day, from the President down to the Deputies. That way, at least, everyone would recognize the person of the State.'

But one of the layabouts, near the coachman, turned round: 'And the fatted ox,* where's that to go?' he said.

A laugh ran round the two long seats. Patissot could see the objection and murmured, 'Perhaps it wouldn't be dignified.'

The gentleman, upon reflection, took the point. 'In that case,' he said, 'I would put them on show somewhere, so that you would be able to look at them all without going to any trouble – on the Arc de Triomphe at the Etoile, for example – and I would make the whole population file past them. That would have a great effect.'

But the layabout turned around once more: 'You'd have to have telescopes to see their mugs.'

The gentleman made no reply; he went on: 'It's like awarding the colours after a battle! You have to have an excuse, to organize something, a little war; and you could give out the standards to the troops afterwards as a reward. I had an idea, myself, which I wrote about to the Minister, but he didn't deign to reply. Since they have chosen the date of the capture of the Bastille, they should organize a re-enactment of the event; they should have

---

*An ox was often part of the carnival procession on Mardi Gras.

made a Bastille out of cardboard decorated by a scene painter, and hidden the whole *Colonne de Juillet* within its walls.* Then, monsieur, the troops could have attacked; that would have been a great spectacle and at the same time it would have been instructive to see the army itself overturning the ramparts of tyranny. Then it would be set alight, that Bastille; and in the midst of the flames the column would have appeared bearing the spirit of Liberty, symbol of a new order and the enfranchisement of the people.'

By now everyone on the top deck was listening to him, and they thought his idea excellent. An old man affirmed: 'It's a grand idea, monsieur, and one that does you credit. It is a pity that the government did not take it up.'

A young man declared that they should give recitals in the streets of Barbier's 'Iambs',† by actors, to teach the people about art and liberty simultaneously.

These suggestions aroused enthusiasm. Everyone wanted to say something; their brains were afire. A passing barrel organ started playing the 'Marseillaise', the working man sang out the words, and everyone, all together, shouted the refrain. The impassioned pace of the song and its furious rhythm inflamed the coachman, and he whipped his horses until they were galloping. Monsieur Patissot was bawling at the top of his voice and slapping his thighs, and the travellers inside the coach, appalled, were wondering what storm had broken over their heads.

At last they stopped, and Monsieur Patissot, considering his neighbour to be a man of initiative, consulted him on the preparations he was intending to make: 'Some lanterns and some flags,

---

* This column in the middle of the Place de la Bastille is over fifty metres high.
† Auguste Barbier (1805–82), a popular poet who wrote lively satirical verse.

that's all very well,' he said, 'but I would like something better.'

The other thought for a long time, but came up with nothing. So, as a desperate measure, Monsieur Patissot bought three flags and four lanterns.

VII
A sad story

To recover from the exhaustion of the public holiday, Monsieur Patissot thought up the idea of peacefully spending the following Sunday sitting somewhere to contemplate nature.

Wanting a open skyline, he chose the Saint-Germain terrace. It was after lunch when he set out, and when he had gone round the Museum of Ancient History to salve his conscience, for he understood nothing at all, he stood rapt with admiration at this endless promenade from which you can make out in the distance Paris, all the surrounding region, all the plains, all the villages, the woods, the ponds, even the towns, and the great bluish serpent with innumerable bends, that gentle and lovely river which passes through the heart of France: the Seine.

In the far distance, turning blue from the light mists, incalculably far off, he could make out little areas like white spots on the sides of the green hills. And thinking that over there on these almost invisible dots men like him were living, working, enduring, he pondered for the first time how small the world was. He said to himself that, out in space, other dots yet more indistinguishable, universes still bigger than our own must be supporting perhaps more perfect races! But the vastness of it made him dizzy, and he stopped thinking of these things which disturbed his mind. Then he ambled along the broad terrace, a little languid, as though crushed by too weighty thoughts.

When he reached the end he sat on a bench. A man was there

already, his two hands crossed on his walking stick and his chin on his hands, in an attitude of deep meditation. However, Patissot belonged to a race who cannot spend three seconds beside their fellow man without speaking to him. First, he looked at his neighbour, he coughed, then suddenly asked: 'Monsieur, would you be able to tell me the name of the village I can see over there?'

The man lifted his head and, in a sad voice, replied, 'It's Sartrouville.'

Then he fell silent. So Patissot, contemplating the immense view of the terrace shaded by hundred-year-old trees, feeling in his lungs the great breath of the forest rustling behind him, rejuvenated by the scent of spring in the woods and the broad countryside, gave an abrupt little laugh and, a gleam in his eye, said, 'This is lovely shade for lovers.'

His neighbour turned to him with a desperate air., 'If I was in love, monsieur, I would throw myself in the river.'

Patissot, not sharing this point of view at all, protested, 'Hey! You say that very easily; and why is that?'

'Because it's already cost me too dear to begin again.'

'I say! If you've made a fool of yourself, you always pay a price for it.'

But the other sighed sadly.

'No, monsieur, I didn't do anything; events conspired against me, that's all.'

Patissot, who scented a good story, went on: 'All the same, we can't live like clergymen, it goes against nature.'

Then the good fellow raised his eyes to the sky pitifully. 'That's true, monsieur; but if priests were men as others are, my disasters wouldn't have happened. I am an enemy of ecclesiastical celibacy, monsieur, and I have good reason for it.'

Patissot, thoroughly interested, pressed him: 'Would it be

indiscreet to ask you ...'

'Good Lord, no! Here's my story. I am Norman, monsieur. My father was a miller at Darnetal, near Rouen, and when he died we, my brother and I, who were still small children, were left in the care of our uncle, a good, stout priest from the Pays de Caux. He brought us up, monsieur, educated us, then sent us both to Paris to look for suitable positions.

'My brother was twenty-one, and I was twenty-two. We had settled in the same rooms to save money, and we were living there peacefully when the adventure I'm going to tell you about happened.

'One evening, as I was coming home, I met a young woman in the street who very much appealed to me. She was just to my taste: rather rounded, monsieur, and a good-natured air. I didn't dare speak to her, naturally, but I gave her a meaningful look. The next day I found her in the same place. As I was timid, I just bowed; she responded with a little smile, and the following day I spoke to her.

'She was called Victorine and she was a seamstress in a ready-made dress shop. I was pretty sure at once that she had stolen my heart.

'I said to her, "Mademoiselle, it seems to me I can't live without you." She lowered her eyes and didn't answer, so I took her hand, and I felt her squeeze mine. I was ensnared, monsieur; but I didn't know how to proceed because of my brother. Upon my word, I had just decided to tell him everything when he spoke first. He was in love as well. So we agreed to take another flat, but without breathing a word to my uncle, who was still sending his letters to my address. So that is what we did, and a week later Victorine gave a house-warming party at my place. We arranged a little dinner, my brother brought the girl he had met and, in the evening, when my girlfriend had cleared everything up, we finally took possession of our home …

'We had been sleeping for perhaps an hour when a violent ring of the bell woke me up. I looked at the clock: three in the morning. I put on some trousers and rushed to the door, saying to myself, "It's some kind of disaster, it must be …" It was my uncle, monsieur … he had on his travelling coat, and his suitcase was in his hand.

'"Yes, it's me, my boy; I came to surprise you and to spend a few days in Paris. The Bishop has given me some leave."

'He kissed me on both cheeks, came in, shut the door. I was more dead than alive, monsieur. But just as he was about to go into my bedroom, I practically flung myself on his neck: "No, not there, uncle, this way, this way."

'And I made him go into the dining room. Do you see my predicament? What could I do? … He said to me, "And where's your brother? Is he asleep? Go and wake him up then."

'I stammered, "No, uncle, he had to spend the night at the shop to meet an urgent order."

'My uncle rubbed his hands. "So, is the work going well?"

'But an idea was coming to me. "You must be hungry, uncle, after your journey."

'"My word, that's true. I wouldn't mind a little snack."

'I rushed to the cupboard (I still had the remains of dinner), and my uncle was a solid trencherman, a real Norman *curé* capable of eating for twelve hours at a stretch. I got out a piece of beef to gain time, because I knew quite well he didn't care for it; then, when he had had enough, I brought out some left-over chicken, a pâté which had hardly been touched, a potato salad, three pots of cream and some good wine which I had put aside for the next day. Ah! monsieur, he nearly fell over backwards: "Heavens above! What a larder!" …

'And I stuffed him, monsieur, I stuffed him! In any case, he couldn't resist. (In the country they used to say he could have swallowed a herd of cattle.)

'By the time he'd devoured the lot it was five o'clock in the morning! I felt as though I was on hot coals. I dragged things out for another hour with coffee and little tots, but in the end he got up. "Let's see your lodgings," he said.

'I was done for, and I followed him, thinking of throwing myself out of the window ... As I went into the bedroom, on the point of fainting, yet expecting I don't know what fluke, a last hope made my heart jump. The grand girl had closed the bed curtains! Ah! Perhaps he wouldn't open them? Alas, monsieur, he went straight up to them, candle in hand, and in one movement he lifted them aside ... The weather was warm, we had taken off the blankets, leaving only the sheet, which she had pulled over her head; but you could see, monsieur, you could see the contours. I was trembling in every limb, my throat tight, suffocating. Then my uncle turned to me, with a broad grin, monsieur, with a broad grin; so much so that I nearly hit the ceiling with astonishment.

'"Ho! Ho! My practical joker," he said. "You didn't want to wake your brother! Well, you'll see how I am going to wake him."

'I saw his hand, his big countryman's hand, rising up and, stifling his laughter, he brought it down like thunder on ... on the contours before us, monsieur.

'There was a terrible cry from the bed, and then something like a storm beneath the sheet! It was moving, it was moving; she could not get free. At last she appeared, almost all of her at once, with eyes like lanterns; and she was looking at my uncle who was backing away, his mouth open, and gasping, monsieur, as if he was going to be ill!

'Then I completely lost my head and I fled ... I wandered about for six days, monsieur, not daring to return home. Finally, when I was brave enough to come back, there was no one there …'

Patissot, shaking with laughter, blurted out, 'I can well believe it!', which silenced his neighbour.

Then, after a second, the good fellow went on, 'I have never seen my uncle since. He disinherited me, convinced that I was taking advantage of my brother's absences to have my fun. I have never seen Victorine since. All my family have turned their back on me, and even my brother, who has profited from the situation since he got a hundred thousand francs on the death of my uncle, seems to think I'm an old libertine. And yet, monsieur, I swear to you that since that moment, never … never … never! … You see, there are moments you never forget.'

'And what are you doing here?' asked Patissot.

The other, with an all-embracing glance, looked round the horizon, as though he feared being overheard by some unknown ear, then murmured, with terror in his voice:

'I'm fleeing from women, monsieur!'

VIII
An attempt at love

Many poets believe nature is incomplete without woman, and from that no doubt come all the floral comparisons in their verse which make of our natural companion, in turns, a rose, a violet, a tulip, etc., etc. The emotional need which comes over us at the hour of dusk, when the evening mist starts to float over the hill-sides and when all the scents of the earth intoxicate us, overflows clumsily into lyrical outbursts; and Monsieur Patissot, like others, was gripped by a fever of amorous feelings, of sweet kisses reciprocated along paths streaming with sunshine, of pressed hands, of plump waistlines bending beneath his embrace.

He was beginning to envisage love as unbounded pleasure and, when he was daydreaming, he would thank the great Unknown for having put so much charm into man's caresses. But he needed a partner, and he didn't know where to meet her. On the advice of a friend he went to the Folies-Bergère. There he saw a whole range of them; but now he found he was quite perplexed when deciding between them, for the desires in his heart were made up, above all, of flights of poetry, and poetry did not seem to be the speciality of these ladies of the charcoaled eyes, who threw him disturbing smiles with the enamel of their false teeth.

At last his choice fell on a young beginner who seemed poor and timid and whose sad look seemed to suggest a nature fairly easily poeticized.

He arranged to meet her the next day at nine o'clock, at the Saint-Lazare station.

She didn't turn up, but she was kind enough to send a friend instead.

This was a big redhead, dressed patriotically in three colours and covered with an enormous tunnel-like hat, with her head in the centre of it. Monsieur Patissot, rather disappointed, nevertheless accepted this substitute, and they left for Maisons-Laffitte, where there were to be regattas and a big Venetian fête.

As soon as they were in the carriage, already occupied by two gentlemen wearing the ribbons of an order in their buttonholes and three ladies who must have been at least marchionesses, so much were they on their dignity, the big redhead, who answered to the name Octavie, announced to Patissot in a parrot-like voice that she was a very good girl, that she loved a good laugh and adored the countryside, because you picked flowers and ate fried fish there; and she laughed with a laugh shrill enough to break windows, familiarly calling her companion 'my big wolf'.

Shame overcame Patissot, whose position as a government employee demanded a certain reserve. But Octavie fell silent, casting sidelong looks at her female neighbours, consumed by the unreasonable desire which haunts all tarts to make the acquaintance of respectable women. After five minutes she thought she had found a way and, pulling *Gil Blas* out of her pocket,* she politely offered it to one of the astounded ladies, who refused it with a movement of the head. The big redhead, hurt, fired off a number of words with double meanings, talking of women who put on airs without being any better than anyone else, and occasionally she even threw out a swear word which had the effect of a failed firecracker in the midst of the travellers' icy dignity.

At last they arrived. Patissot wanted to get to the shady corners of the park straight away, hoping that the melancholy of the woods would soften his friend's irritable humour. But it produced a different effect. As soon as she was among the leaves and she saw the grass she began to sing at the top of her voice scraps of opera that lay about in her feather-head memory, doing trills, going from *Robert le Diable* to *La Muette*,† and especially favouring sentimentally poetic parts, the last verses of which she would coo with a sound as piercing as a gimlet:

> And as for me, joyful at the return of spring,
> I began to sing as you sing at twenty.

All of a sudden she was hungry and wanted to go back. Patissot, who was still waiting for the hoped-for affection, tried in vain to keep her. Then she became angry.

---

* *Gil Blas* had a reputation for much greater licence in its articles and stories than did *Le Gaulois*, in which this story first appeared (Maupassant was shortly to write for *Gil Blas* also); respectable women would not be seen reading it.
† Well-known operas by Meyerbeer and Auber.

'I'm not here to be pestered, am I?'

And they had to get to the Petit Havre restaurant, right close to the spot where the regattas were to be.

She ordered a meal as though she would never stop, a succession of dishes enough to feed a regiment. Then, unable to wait, she demanded an hors-d'oeuvre. A tin of sardines appeared; she threw herself upon it, and it seemed the tin itself would go down; but when she had eaten two or three of the oily little fish she declared she was no longer hungry and wanted to go and see the preparations for the races.

Patissot, in despair and famished in his turn, absolutely refused to get up. She went off alone, promising to come back for dessert; and he began to eat, silently and alone, not knowing how to bring this intractable character around to realizing his dream.

Since she did not return, he set out to look for her.

She had found some friends, a group of half-naked oarsmen, red to their ears and gesticulating, loudly arranging all the details of the races in front of the house of Fournaise the boatbuilder.

Two men of respectable appearance, no doubt judges, were listening to them attentively. As soon as she saw Patissot, Octavie, who was draped over the dark arm of a tall devil who certainly possessed more biceps than brains, said a few words in his ear. The other replied, 'All right.'

And she came back to the clerk full of joy, bright-eyed, almost affectionate.

'I would like to go out in a boat,' she said.

Happy to see her so charming, he consented to this new wish and got hold of a craft.

But she obstinately refused to watch the regatta, despite Patissot's wishes.

'I would rather be alone with you, my wolf.'

His heart leaped ... At last! ...

He took off his coat and began to row furiously.

A huge old mill, whose worm-eaten wheels were suspended over the water, straddled a little branch of the river with its two arches. They passed slowly underneath and, when they were on the other side, they saw before them a charming little bit of river, shaded by large trees which formed a sort of vault above them. The little tributary unwound, turned, zigzagged to the left, to the right, constantly revealing new vistas, large meadows on one side and, on the other, a hillside quite covered in chalets. They passed in front of a bathing place, almost buried in greenery, a charming and pastoral corner, where gentlemen in light gloves, beside flower-garlanded ladies, were going in for all the absurd gaucherie of the elegant in the countryside.

She cried out in delight.

'We can bathe there shortly!'

Then, further off, in a sort of bay, she wanted to stop: 'Come here, big boy, right close to me.'

She put her arms round his neck and, her head leaning against Patissot's shoulder, she murmured, 'How cosy! How nice it is on the water!'

Patissot, indeed, was overflowing with happiness, and he thought of those stupid oarsmen who, without ever being aware of the pervasive charm of the banks and the delicate grace of the reeds, are always going from the dive where they have lunch to the dive where they have dinner, panting, sweating and brutalized by exercise.

But, being so cosy, he went to sleep.

When he awoke ... he was alone. At first he called; no one answered. Anxiously he got out on to the bank, fearing now that some accident might have befallen.

Then, far off and coming towards him, he saw a long, slim skiff which four rowers black as Negroes were making speed along like an arrow. It came closer, skimming over the water — a woman was steering ... Heavens! You might almost think ... It was her! To keep the rhythm of the oars she was singing a rowing song in her shrill voice, which she interrupted for a moment when she was in front of Patissot. Then, blowing him a kiss, she shouted to him:

'Get away, you great booby!'

IX
A dinner and a few ideas

On the occasion of the national public holiday, Monsieur Perdrix (Antoine), head of Monsieur Patissot's office, had been made a Chevalier of the Legion d'Honneur. He had thirty years under previous regimes to his credit and ten years of service to the present government. His employees, though they murmured somewhat at being thus rewarded through the person of their superior, thought it right to present him with a cross ornamented with false diamonds, and the new Chevalier, not wanting to be behindhand, invited them all to dine on the following Sunday at his property in Asnières.

The house, lit up with Moorish ornaments, had the look of a *café-concert*, but it was its situation that gave it value, for the railway line, cutting through the garden across its whole width, passed within twenty metres of the steps. On the obligatory circle of lawn was a fountain made of Roman cement containing some goldfish, and a jet of water, perfectly resembling a syringe, occasionally threw microscopic rainbows into the air, to the wonderment of visitors.

The supply for this pastoral water system was a constant

preoccupation for Monsieur Perdrix, who sometimes got up at five in the morning to fill the tank. Then he would pump determinedly, in shirt sleeves, his big belly hanging out of his trousers, so that he could have the satisfaction of turning on playing fountains when he returned from the office, imagining that it spread cool throughout the garden.

On the evening of the formal dinner all those invited, one after another, enthused about the position of the estate. Every time they heard a train coming from far off, Monsieur Perdrix would announce its destination: Saint-Germain, Le Havre, Cherbourg or Dieppe, and as a joke they would wave to the travellers leaning out of the doors.

The entire office was there. First of all there was Monsieur Capitaine, deputy head; Monsieur Patissot, chief clerk; then Messieurs Sombreterre and Vallin, elegant young employees who only came to the office at times of day that suited them; finally Monsieur Rade, known throughout the Ministry for the senseless opinions he aired, and the dispatch clerk, Monsieur Boivin.

Monsieur Rade was considered to be a character. Some called him whimsical or an idealistic visionary; others a revolutionary; everyone concurred in saying he lacked tact. Now old, small and thin, with bright eyes and long white hair, all his life he had expressed the deepest scorn for administrative work. A great reader, always looking at books, with a nature that forever rebelled against everything, a seeker after truth and scourge of current prejudices, he had a neat and paradoxical way of expressing his opinions which silenced the complacent fools and the malcontents without their knowing why. People said, 'That old madman Rade', or else 'That brainless Rade', and the slowness of his promotion seemed to justify the mediocre upstarts against him. The independence of his speech quite often made his colleagues quake, and they would ask each other in terror how he managed to keep his job. As soon as they were at table Monsieur Perdrix, in a heartfelt little speech, thanked his 'fellow workers', promised them his protection which would be the more effective with the increase in his authority, and he wound up with an emotional peroration in which he thanked and glorified the just and liberal government, which knew how to seek out merit in the humble.

Monsieur Capitaine, deputy head, replied on behalf of the office, congratulated, complimented, hailed, exalted and sang the praises of everyone, and frenetic applause greeted these pieces of eloquence. After which they set seriously to eating.

All went well until the dessert, since the threadbare nature of the conversation bothered no one. But with coffee a discussion came up which suddenly unleashed Monsieur Rade, who started to go beyond the pale.

They were talking about love, naturally; a breath of chivalry was going to the heads of this roomful of bureaucrats, and they were extravagantly praising woman's superior beauty, her delicacy of mind, her talent for the exquisite, the sureness of her judgement and her fine sentiments. Monsieur Rade began to protest, energetically denying to the sex described as 'fair' all the qualities attributed to it, and to general indignation he quoted authorities:

'Schopenhauer, gentlemen, Schopenhauer, a great philosopher venerated in Germany. This is what he says:

'"Man's intelligence must have been well obscured by love for him to have called fair this sex which is small in size, narrow-shouldered, large-hipped and short-legged. Its entire beauty, indeed, resides in the instinct for love. Instead of calling it fair, it would have been more just to call it unaesthetic. Women have no more feeling or intellectual appreciation of music than they have of poetry or the plastic arts; in them it is only pure mimicry, pure pretext, pure affectation exploited in their desire to please.'"*

'The man who said that is a fool,' declared Monsieur Sombreterre.

Monsieur Rade, smiling, went on, 'And Rousseau, monsieur? This is his opinion:

'"Women in general love no art, have no knowledge of any and have no genius."'

Monsieur Sombreterre disdainfully shrugged his shoulders: 'Rousseau is as stupid as the other one, that's all.'

Monsieur Rade was still smiling. 'And Lord Byron, who loved women all the same, monsieur, this is what he said:

'"They should be well fed and well clothed, but they should not mix with society. They should also be taught religion, but should remain ignorant of poetry and politics, and should only read pious books and cookery books."'

Monsieur Rade went on, 'Consider, messieurs, that they all study painting and music. Yet not one has produced a good picture or a remarkable opera! Why, messieurs? Because they are the *sexus sequior*, the second sex in every way, made to stay at a distance and in the background.'

Monsieur Patissot was getting angry: 'And Madame Sand, monsieur?'

'An exception, monsieur, an exception. I will quote yet another passage from another great philosopher, English this one, Herbert Spencer. Here it is:

---

* Maupassant quotes accurately from Jean Bourdeau's translation *Pensées et fragments* (Germer Baillère, 1880, the same year as this story). I have translated that translation, rather than using a contemporary English translation of Schopenhauer, since that is what Maupassant was familiar with. Rousseau and Byron, which follow, were used as examples by Schopenhauer.

"'Each sex is capable, under the influence of a particular stimulus, of manifesting faculties normally reserved for the other. Thus, to take an extreme case, special stimulation can produce milk in male breasts; during famines, small children deprived of their mother have been observed to be saved in this way. Nevertheless we would not number this ability to produce milk as being among the male attributes. In the same way, feminine intelligence which, in certain cases, will give rise to a superior product, should be ignored in evaluating feminine nature, being a social factor . . .'"

Monsieur Patissot, wounded in all his innate chivalrous instincts, declared, 'You are not French, monsieur. French gallantry is one of the forms of patriotism.'

Monsieur Rade returned the shot. 'I have very little patriotism, monsieur, as little as possible.'

A chill spread through the company, but he quietly went on:

'Do you agree with me that war is a monstrous thing; that this custom of cutting people's throats amounts to a permanent state of savagery; that it is odious – since the only real good is life – to see governments, whose duty is to protect the existence of their subjects, obstinately seeking the means of destruction? Is it not so? Well, if war is a thing of horror, might patriotism not be the fundamental idea which maintains it? When a murderer kills he has one idea: to steal. When a brave man, with a bayonet thrust, splits open another honest man, perhaps a father of a family or a great artist, what thought is he obeying?'

Everyone felt deeply upset.

'When one thinks things like that one does not say them in company.'

Monsieur Patissot went on: 'Besides, monsieur, there are principles that all honest people recognize.'

Monsieur Rade asked, 'What are they?'

Then Monsieur Patissot announced solemnly, 'Morality, monsieur.'

Monsieur Rade was beaming; he cried: 'One example, messieurs, one tiny example. What opinion do you have of these gentlemen in silk caps who ply the nice trade – you know – on the outer boulevards and who live off it?'

Expressions of distaste ran round the table.

'Well, messieurs, only a century ago, when an elegant gentleman very punctilious in matters of honour, had for his ... friend ... a "very beautiful and honest lady of high birth", he would be very much inclined to live at her expense, messieurs, and even to completely ruin her. This was thought to be a delightful game. Therefore moral principles are not fixed ... and so ...'

Monsieur Perdrix, visibly embarrassed, stopped him. 'You are undermining the foundations of society, Monsieur Rade. There must always be principles. Just as in politics we have here Monsieur Sombreterre who is a Legitimist, Monsieur Vallin an Orléanist, Monsieur Patissot and myself Republicans, we have very different principles, do we not, and yet we understand each other very well because we do have them.'

But Monsieur Rade cried out, 'Me too. I have them, Messieurs, I have very firm ones.'

Monsieur Patissot raised his head and said coldly, 'I would be pleased to hear them, monsieur.'

Monsieur Rade needed no encouragement: 'Here they are, monsieur:

'First principle: government by one is a monstrosity.

'Second principle: Partial suffrage is an injustice.

'Third principle: Universal suffrage is an idiocy.

'Indeed to hand over millions of men, men of superior intelligence, scholars, even geniuses, to the caprice, the good will of a creature who, in a moment of gaiety, madness, drunkenness or passion would not hesitate to sacrifice everything to his excited imagination, would spend the wealth of the country painfully amassed by everyone, would have millions of men cut up on battle fields, etc., etc., seems to me, a simple thinker, a monstrous aberration.

'But if we admit that the country should govern itself, to exclude on a debatable pretext one part of its citizens from the administration of its affairs is so flagrant an injustice that it seems to me useless to discuss it further.

'That leaves universal suffrage. You will agree with me that men of genius are rare, will you not? To be generous, let us suppose there are five in France at this moment. Let us add, still to be generous, two hundred very talented men, a thousand others with different kinds of talents, and ten thousand who are superior in one way or another. That gives us a general staff of eleven thousand two hundred minds. After which you have the army of the mediocre, followed by the multitude of idiots. Since the mediocre and the idiots always form the immense majority, it is out of the question that they would be able to elect an intelligent government.

'To be fair I will add that, logically, universal suffrage seems to me to be the only acceptable principle, but it is unworkable, and here's why.

'To combine in the government all the vital forces of a country, to represent all interests, to take into account all rights, is an idealistic dream but not a very practical one, because the only force you could measure is precisely the one which ought to be the most neglected, the power of foolishness, numbers. According to your method the unintelligent majority takes precedence over

71

genius, scholarship, all acquired knowledge, riches, industry, etc., etc. If you were able to give a member of the Institute ten thousand votes against ten votes for his tenant farmer, you would have more or less brought the forces into equilibrium and arrived at a national representation which was really representative of all the powers of the nation. But I defy you to do that.

'These are my conclusions: In former times, when you couldn't enter one of the professions you became a photographer; today you become a deputy in Parliament. A power made up like that will always be pitifully incapable; but incapable of doing harm as well as incapable of doing good. A tyrant, on the other hand, if he is stupid, can do a great deal of harm, and if it turns out he is intelligent (which is incredibly rare) a great deal of good.

'I cannot decide between these forms of government, and I declare myself an anarchist; that is to say in favour of the most efficient power, the most detached, the most liberal in the broad sense of the word, and at the same time revolutionary; that is to say the eternal enemy of that same power, which can only be in any case totally defective. There you are.'

Cries of indignation rose round the table, and all of them, Legitimist, Orléanist, Republican by necessity, really saw red. Monsieur Patissot, in particular, was gasping and, turning to Monsieur Rade, declared: 'Then, monsieur, you believe in nothing.'

The other simply replied, 'No, monsieur.'

The anger that aroused the entire company prevented Monsieur Rade from continuing and Monsieur Perdrix, becoming the head again, closed the discussion.

'Enough, gentlemen, please. We all have our own opinions and we are not inclined to change them.'

They approved these impartial words. But Monsieur Rade,

always rebellious, wanted to have the last word.

'All the same I do have a morality,' he said. 'It is very simple and always applicable; one sentence sums it up, and this is it: Do as you would be done by. I challenge you to find fault with it, while I can be sure of demolishing in three arguments the most sacred of your principles.'

This time there was no reply. But as they went back in the evening two by two, everyone said to his companion, 'No, really, Monsieur Rade goes a great deal too far. He certainly has a bee in his bonnet. They should make him deputy head at Charenton.'*

X
A public meeting

On both sides of a door above which the word 'Dancing' was displayed in garish letters, large posters in violent red announced that on that Sunday this place of popular entertainment would serve another purpose.

Monsieur Patissot, who was taking a stroll like a good bourgeois while he digested his lunch and was going gently in the direction of the station, stopped, his eye caught by the scarlet colour, and he read:

PUBLIC MEETING

International General Association
for Promoting the Rights of Women

CENTRAL COMMITTEE HEADQUARTERS PARIS
BIG PUBLIC MEETING

Under the Presidency of the free-thinker Citizen Zöe Lamour and the
Russian nihilist Citizen Eva Schourine,
with the assistance of
a delegation of women citizens of the free circle of

---

* The lunatic asylum.

73

Independent Thought and a group of citizen members.

Citizen Césarine Brau and Citizen Sapience Cornut, back from his exile, will address the meeting.

ENTRANCE: 1 FRANC

An old lady with glasses, sitting at a carpet-covered table, was taking the money. Monsieur Patissot went in.

In the hall, already almost full, the smell of wet dog that always comes from old maids' skirts was drifting about, together with remnants of the dubious perfumes of public dance halls.

After searching carefully, Monsieur Patissot found an empty seat in the second row between an old gentleman wearing a ribbon of the Legion d'Honneur and a little woman in working clothes, with an impassioned look and a mottled swelling on her cheek.

All the members of the executive were there.

Citizen Zöe Lamour, a pretty, plump brunette wearing red flowers in her black hair, was presiding together with a thin little blonde, the Russian nihilist Citizen Eva Schourine.

Just below them the famous Citizen Césarine Brau, nicknamed 'Man-killer', and she too was pretty, was sitting next to Citizen Sapience Cornut, returned from exile. The latter, an out-and-out old faithful with a ferocious appearance, was looking at the hall as a cat looks at an aviary full of birds, and his clenched fists were resting on his knees.

On the right a delegation of ancient women citizens deprived of husbands, shrivelled by celibacy and fuming at the delay, were stationed opposite a group of citizens who were reformers of humanity, who had never cut either their beards or their hair, no doubt to show the infinite reach of their aspirations.

It was a mixed audience.

The women, who were in the majority, belonged to the caste of concierges and shopkeepers who shut on Sundays. The typical inconsolable old maid (known as the old bag) appeared every-where among the red faces of the bourgeois women. Three school-boys were talking quietly in a corner, come there to be among women. A few families had come in out of curiosity. But in the first row a Negro in yellow drill, a curly, magnificent Negro, was look-ing determinedly at the platform with a smile from ear to ear and a silent, contained laugh that made his white teeth sparkle in his black face. He laughed without a movement of his body, as though transported and enchanted. Why was he there? It was a mystery. Did he think he was at a show? Or else was he saying to himself in his frizzy African nut, 'Really, really, they are too comic, these jokers; you would never find their like below the Equator.'

Citizen Zöe Lamour opened the meeting with a little speech.

She recalled the slavery of woman since the world began; her humble role, ever heroic, her constant devotion to all great ideas. She compared her to earlier populations, the populations of the time of kings and of the aristocracy, calling her 'the eternal martyr' for whom every man is master; and, in a great lyrical movement, she cried out, 'The people have had their 1789 – let us have ours; oppressed man created his Revolution; the captive sundered his chains, the wrathful slave rose up. Women, let us imitate our despots. Let us make a revolution; let us tear asunder the ancient chain of marriage and of slavery; let us march on to the conquest of our rights; let us too have our revolution.'

She sat down to thunderous applause, and the Negro, mad with joy, began beating his forehead against his knees, uttering piercing shrieks.

The Russian nihilist Citizen Eva Schourine got up and, in a ferocious and penetrating voice, declared, 'I am a Russian. I have raised the standard of rebellion. This hand has struck the oppressors of my country; and I declare to you, Frenchwomen listening to me, I am ready, under any sun, anywhere in the universe, to strike against male tyranny, to avenge everywhere the unbearable oppression of woman.'

There was a great tumult of approval, and Citizen Sapience Cornut himself got to his feet and touched his yellow beard to her avenging hand.

It was then that the proceedings took on a really international character. The women citizen delegates from foreign powers got up one after another, bringing the support of their countries. A German woman spoke first. She was very fat, with tow-like vegetation on her cranium, and jabbered in a thick voice:

'I vant to say vot glatness zere vas in olt Germany vhen ve knew of ze great movement of ze Barisian vomen. Our breasts' – she beat her own, which shuddered under the impact – 'our breasts trempled, our ... our ... I do not spik vell, but ve are viz you.'

An Italian, a Spanish and a Swedish woman said much the same with surprising turns of phrase, and to end up a very tall Englishwoman, with teeth like garden tools, expressed herself in these terms: 'I too wish to convey the participation of a free England to the so ... so ... very picturesque manifestation of the feminine population of France in favour of the emancipation of this feminine country. Hip! Hip! Hurrah!'*

This time the Negro let out such cries of enthusiasm, with such extravagant gestures of satisfaction (throwing his legs over the backs of the benches and furiously slapping his thighs), that two stewards were obliged to calm him down.

---

* It is unfortunately impossible to reproduce in an English translation Maupassant's wickedly effective French spoken with a truly execrable English accent. He claimed not to speak English, but he certainly had an ear for it.

Patissot's neighbour whispered, 'Hysterics! They are all hysterics!'

Patissot, thinking he was being spoken to, turned round, 'I beg your pardon?'

The gentleman apologized. 'I am sorry, I wasn't speaking to you. I was just saying that all these crazy women are hysterics!'

Monsieur Patissot, quite astonished, asked, 'Do you know them then?'

'A little, monsieur! Zöe Lamour has done her noviciate to become a nun. That's one of them. Eva Schourine has been prosecuted for arson and diagnosed as mad. That's another. Césarine Brau is just a schemer who wants to be talked about. I can see three more of them over there who have been in my department at X— Hospital. As for all the old battleaxes around us, I need hardly say a word.'

But there was 'shush' from all sides. Citizen Sapience Cornut, returned from exile, stood up. First, he rolled his eyes fearfully, then, in a hollow voice like the roaring of the wind in a cave, he began:

'There are words which are as great as principles, as brilliant as suns, reverberating like thunder: Liberty! Equality! Fraternity! These are the people's banners. Under their furls we have marched into battle against tyranny. O women, it is your turn to brandish them like weapons as you march to the conquest of independence. Be free, free in love, in the home, in the nation. Become our equals at the fireside, our equals in the streets and especially our equals in politics and before the law. Fraternity! Be our sisters, confidantes in our glorious projects, our valiant companions. Be, become, truly half of humanity instead of just a fragment of it.'

And he launched into transcendental politics, developing

plans of world scope, talking of the soul of societies, predicting a universal Republic built on the three unshakeable bases: liberty, equality, fraternity.

When he was silent the hall nearly collapsed under the weight of the bravos. Monsieur Patissot, astounded, turned to his neighbour. 'Isn't he a little mad?'

The old man replied, 'No, monsieur, there are millions like that. It's one of the effects of education.'

Patissot did not understand. 'Education?'

'Yes; now they know how to read and write, their latent stupidity can find expression.'

'But, monsieur, do you believe that education ...?'

'I beg your pardon, monsieur, I am a liberal myself. This is all I want to say: you have a watch, don't you? Well, break a spring, take it to Citizen Cornut and ask him to mend it. He will reply, swearing, that he is not a watchmaker. But if something goes wrong in this infinitely complicated machine called France, he believes he is the most capable man to repair it on the spot. Forty thousand loudmouths of his type think the same and are constantly saying so. I say, monsieur, that so far we are lacking a new governing class, that is to say men born of fathers accustomed to power, brought up with this idea, specially educated for the job of government in the same way young people heading for the Ecole Polytechnique are specially educated.'

Numerous shushes once more interrupted him. A young man with a melancholy air was on the platform. He began:

'Ladies, I asked to speak to take issue with your theories. To demand for women civil rights equal to men's is the same as demanding an end to your power. The very appearance of a woman shows that she is meant for neither hard physical work nor lengthy intellectual effort. Her role is different but no less beautiful. She puts poetry into life. With the power of her grace, a ray from her eyes, the charm of her smile, she rules man, who rules the world. Man has strength, which you cannot take from him, but you have the power of seduction which makes a captive of strength. What are you complaining about? Since the world began you have been sovereigns and rulers. Nothing can be done without you. It is for you that all beautiful works are created.

'But the day you become our civil and political equals you will become our rivals. So take care not to spoil the charm which constitutes your strength. If you do, since we are undeniably the more vigorous and the more talented at science and the arts, your inferiority will appear, and you will really become the oppressed.

'You have the best role, ladies, because for us you are the attraction of life, the perpetual illusion, the eternal reward for our efforts. So don't seek to change anything. You will not succeed in any case.'

But he was interrupted by catcalls. He got down.

Patissot's neighbour stood up. 'A bit romantic, that young man, but at least he's sensible. Would you like to come and have a beer, monsieur?'

'With pleasure.'

They made their way out, while Citizen Césarine Brau was getting ready to reply.

'Les Dimanches d'un bourgeois de Paris' was first published from 31 May to 16 August 1880 in Le Gaulois. *It has never before been translated into English.*

A Page of Unpublished History

Everyone knows Pascal's famous phrase about the grain of sand which altered the fate of the universe by changing Cromwell's luck.[*] In the same way, among those great accidents in events which govern man and the world, a very small fact, a woman's despairing gesture, decided the fate of Europe by saving the life of the young Napoleon Bonaparte, he who was the great Napoleon.

This is a page of unknown history (for everything which touches the existence of that extraordinary being is historical), a real Corsican drama which was almost fatal to the young officer, then on leave in his homeland.

The story which follows is authentic in every detail. I have written it as if from dictation, without changing anything, without omitting anything, without trying to make it more 'literary' or more dramatic, simply leaving the facts to stand quite alone, quite bare, quite simple, with all the names, all the movements of the characters and the words they spoke.

Perhaps a more composed narrative would be more pleasing; but this is history, and you do not touch history. I got these details directly from the only man who could have had them from the source and whose testimony directed the inquiry that was opened into these same facts around 1853 with the aim of executing the

---

[*] Pascal was referring to a grain of sand in Oliver Cromwell's ureter, which caused his death and thus re-established the monarchy.

80

bequests laid down by the Emperor as he was dying on Saint Helena.

In fact, three days before his death Napoleon added a codicil to his will containing the following provisions. He wrote:

> I bequeath 20,000 francs to the inhabitant of Bocognano who got me out of the hands of the brigands who wanted to murder me;
>
> 10,000 francs to Monsieur Vizzavona, the only member of that family who was on my side;
>
> 100,000 to Monsieur Jerome Levy;
>
> 100,000 to Monsieur Costa;
>
> 20,000 francs to the Abbé Reccho.

It seems that an old memory of his youth had come into his mind in these last moments. After so many years and so many extraordinary adventures, the impression left on him by one of the first shocks of his life still remained strong enough to stay with him, even on his deathbed. This was the far-off vision which was obsessing him when he decided to leave these final gifts to the devoted partisan whose name escaped his enfeebled memory and to the friends who had helped him in terrible situations.

Louis XVI had just died. Corsica was governed at that time by General Paoli, a violent and energetic man, a devoted Royalist who hated the Revolution, while Napoleon Bonaparte, a young artillery officer then on leave in Ajaccio, was using his influence and that of his family in favour of new ideas.

Cafés did not exist in this still wild country, and in the evenings Napoleon gathered together his partisans in a bedroom where they would talk, make plans, take decisions and peer into the future, all the while eating figs and drinking wine.

There was already animosity between the young Napoleon and General Paoli. This is how it had come about. Paoli, having received the order to conquer the Île de la Madeleine, entrusted this mission to Colonel Cesari, while telling him, so they say, to make sure the attempt failed. Napoleon, appointed Lieutenant-Colonel of the National Guard in the regiment commanded by Colonel Quenza, took part in this expedition and protested vigorously afterwards at the manner in which it had been conducted, openly accusing his seniors of having lost deliberately.

It was a short time after this that the Republic's representatives, among whom happened to be Saliceti, were sent to Bastia. On hearing of their arrival Napoleon wanted to join them and, to undertake this journey, he sent for his trusted man from Bocognano, one of his most faithful supporters, Santo-Bonelli, known as Riccio, who was to be his guide.

The two of them left on horseback, going in the direction of Corte, where General Paoli was to be found, since Bonaparte wanted to see him on the way. He did not then know of his chief's involvement in the conspiracy against France and was even defending him against whispered suspicions, and the hostility that had grown up between them, though already sharp, had not yet exploded.

The young Napoleon got off his horse in the courtyard of the house where Paoli was living and, giving his mount into the care of Santo-Riccio, wanted to go at once to the general. But as he was going up the stairs a person he approached informed him that at that very moment a sort of council was taking place, formed of the main Corsican leaders, all opponents of Republican ideas. Perturbed, Napoleon was trying to find out more when one of the conspirators left the meeting. Approaching him, Bonaparte asked, 'Well?' The other, believing him to be an ally, replied, 'It's done. We are going to proclaim independence and separate ourselves from France, with the help of England.' Napoleon was up in arms, carried away and, stamping his foot, he cried, 'This is treachery, it's infamous!', at which point men appeared, attracted by the noise. It so happened that they were distant relatives of the Bonaparte family. Seeing the danger the young man had put himself in, for Paoli was capable of getting rid of him on the spot and for ever, they surrounded him and compelled him go downstairs again and get on his horse.

He left at once, returning to Ajaccio, still accompanied by Santo-Riccio. As night fell they arrived at the hamlet of Arca-de-Vivario and slept at the house of Curé Arrighi, a relative of Napoleon's. He brought Napoleon up to date with what was happening and asked his advice, for he was an upright man of great judgement and respected throughout Corsica.

Setting out again the next day as soon as dawn broke, they travelled all day and by evening reached the entrance to the village of Bocognano. There Napoleon parted from his guide, asking him to come to look for him in the morning with the horses at the crossroads, and he went on to the hamlet of Pogiola to seek the hospitality of Felix Tusoli, his relative and supporter, whose house was a little further on.

Meanwhile General Paoli had learned of the young Bonaparte's visit and of his violent words when he discovered the plot, so he instructed Mario Peraldi to set out in pursuit of him and to prevent him, at any cost, from reaching Ajaccio or Bastia.

Mario Peraldi reached Bocognano a few hours before Napoleon and went to the house of the Morellis, a powerful family who supported the general. They soon learned that the young officer had arrived in the village, and that he would spend the night at Tusoli's house. When the senior Morelli, an energetic and formidable man, was told of Paoli's orders he promised his envoy that Napoleon would not escape.

At daybreak he had his men posted, covering all the roads and ways out of the village. Bonaparte, accompanied by his host, left to rejoin Santo-Riccio, but Tusoli, who was a little unwell and had his head wrapped in a scarf, left him almost immediately. As soon as the young officer was alone a man came up to him and told him that in a nearby inn some of the general's supporters were to be found, on the way to join him at Corte. Napoleon went there and, finding them all together, told them: 'Go and join your leader. You are doing a grand and noble deed.' But at that moment the Morellis, rushing into the house, threw themselves on him, took him prisoner and carried him off.

Santo-Riccio, who was waiting for him at the crossroads, immediately heard of his arrest, and he ran to a Bonaparte supporter called Vizzavona whom he knew to be capable of helping him and whose house was near the Morellis', where Napoleon was to be locked up.

Santo-Riccio had grasped the extreme gravity of the situation. 'If we don't manage to save him straight away, ' he said, 'he is done for. He may be dead in two hours.'

Vizzavona went off to find the Morellis, adroitly sounded them out and, since they were concealing their true intentions, he persuaded them with skill and eloquence to allow the young man to come to him to have something to eat while they guarded his house.

No doubt the better to hide their plans, they agreed to this, and their leader, the only one who knew what the general wanted, left them to watch the place and went back home to prepare for his departure.

It was this absence which saved the life of the prisoner a few minutes later.

In the meantime Santo-Riccio, with the devotion which comes naturally to Corsicans, showing extraordinary sang-froid and undaunted courage, prepared his companion's rescue. He enlisted the help of two young men, brave and faithful like himself, then, having secretly led them to a garden adjoining the Vizzavona house and hidden them behind a wall, he calmly went to the Morellis and asked their permission to say goodbye to Napoleon, since they were going to take him away.

They granted this favour and as soon as he was with Bonaparte and Vizzavona he explained his plans, hastening the escape, as the slightest delay could be fatal to the young man. So the three of them went into the stable, and in the doorway Vizzavona kissed his guest and said to him, 'May God save you, my poor child, He alone can do it!'

Napoleon and Santo-Riccio crawled out to join the two young men hidden behind the wall. Then, making a dash for it, all three fled as fast as their legs could carry them to a nearby spring hidden among some trees. But they had to pass under the nose of the Morellis who, catching sight of them, set off in pursuit with loud shouts.

The Morelli leader, who had come back home, heard them and, grasping what was going on, hurried off with such a fierce look on his face that his wife, who was related to the Tusolis with whom Bonaparte had spent the night, threw herself at his feet, asking, pleading for the young man's life to be saved. Furiously he pushed her away, and he was rushing outside when she, still on her knees, grabbed him by the legs, encircling them with her arms; then beaten, flung aside, but determinedly hanging on, she pulled her husband on to the floor beside her.

If it had not been for the strength and the courage of that woman the game would have been up for Napoleon. The whole of modern history would therefore have been different. People would not have had to memorize the names of his resounding victories! Millions would not have died under cannon fire! The map of Europe would not be the same! And who knows under what political regime we would be living today?

Meanwhile the Morellis had caught up with the fugitives. Santo-Riccio, undaunted, leaning against the trunk of a chestnut tree, faced up to them, shouting to the two young men to take Bonaparte away. But he refused to abandon his guide, who was shouting and aiming a gun at their enemies: 'Grab him then, the lot of you, seize him, tie him hand and foot!'

But they were caught, surrounded, seized, and a Morelli supporter called Honorato put his gun at Napoleon's temple and shouted, 'Death to the country's betrayer!' But just at that moment the man who had sheltered Bonaparte, Felix Tusoli, warned by an emissary from Santo-Riccio, arrived with his relatives, all armed. Seeing the danger, and recognising his brother-in-law among the men threatening his guest's life, he shouted, aiming his gun at him, 'Honorato, Honorato, it's going to be settled between us!'

The other, surprised, hesitated to shoot, and Santo-Riccio, profiting from the confusion and leaving the two parties to fight or have it out, gripped the still-resisting Napoleon in his arms, dragged him off with the help of the two young men, and they plunged into the brush.

A minute later, the Morelli leader, disencumbered of his wife and in a towering rage, at last rejoined his supporters. But by now the fugitives were making their way on foot across mountains, ravines and dense woods. When they reached safety Santo-Riccio sent back the two young men, who were to meet them again the next day with horses near the Ucciani bridge. As they were leaving Napoleon went up to them.

'I am going to return to France,' he said to them. 'Do you want to come with me? Whatever my fortune might be, you will share it.'

They answered, 'Our lives are yours; do what you will with us here, but we will not leave our village.'

So these two simple and devoted boys returned to Bocognano to find horses, and Bonaparte and Santo-Riccio painfully continued their march amid all the obstructions which make journeys in wild and mountainous countries so hard.

They stopped on the way to break bread with the Mancini family, and in the evening they reached Ucciani, home of the Pozzolis, supporters of the Bonapartes. The next day, when he woke up, Napoleon found the house surrounded by armed men. They were all relatives and friends of his hosts, ready to accompany him and indeed to die for him.

The horses were waiting near the bridge and the little troop set out, escorting the fugitive as far as the outskirts of Ajaccio. When night came Napoleon went into the town and found refuge with the mayor, Monsieur Jean-Jerome Levy, who hid him in a cupboard. This was a wise precaution, for the police arrived the next day. They searched everywhere without finding anything, then calmly went off, put off the scent by the mayor's skilful indignation as he offered his assiduous help to find the young rebel.

That very evening, aboard a gondola, Napoleon was taken to the other side of the bay, handed over to the Costa family of Bastelica, and hidden in the brush. The story of a siege which he is supposed to have endured in the Capitello tower, a thrilling story published by the guides, is pure dramatic invention – to be taken as seriously as most of the information purveyed by these imaginative businessmen.

A few days later Corsican independence was proclaimed, the Bonaparte house was burned, and the fugitive's three sisters were left in the care of the Abbé Reccho.

Then a French frigate, which was collecting the last French supporters on the coast, took Napoleon on board and brought back to the mother country the hunted, fugitive partisan, he who was to become Emperor and the prodigious general whose good fortune astounded the world.

'Une page d'histoire inédite' was first published on 27 October 1880 in Le Gaulois. *It has never before been translated into English.*

Public Opinion

As eleven o'clock had just struck the employees were hurrying to get to their offices, fearing the boss's arrival.

Each glanced quickly at the papers brought in during his absence; then, having changed his jacket or coat for his old working jacket, paid a visit to his neighbour.

Soon there were five of them in the cubicle where Monsieur Bonnenfant the chief clerk worked, and the daily conversation began as usual. Monsieur Perdrix, the filing clerk, was looking for missing papers, while the aspiring deputy chief, Monsieur Piston, an Officer of the Academy,* was smoking his cigarette as he warmed his backside. The elderly dispatch clerk, old Grappe, was offering the traditional pinch of snuff all round, and Monsieur Rade, journalist and bureaucrat, sceptical scoffer and rebel, with the voice of a cricket, a gleam in his eye and abrupt gestures, was having fun scandalizing his audience.

'What's new this morning?' asked Monsieur Bonnenfant.

'My word, nothing at all,' replied Monsieur Piston, 'The papers are still full of details about Russia and the assassination of the Czar.'

The filing clerk, Monsieur Perdrix, raised his head and pronounced with conviction, 'I wish his successor the best of luck, but I wouldn't want to swap places with him.'

Monsieur Rade began to laugh. 'Nor would he!' he said.

---

* A minor decoration awarded to minor civil servants; Maupassant himself had received it.

Old Grappe chimed in, asking in pitiful tones, 'Where will it all end?'

Monsieur Rade interrupted him. 'It will never end, Daddy Grappe. It's only us who will come to an end. Ever since there have been kings there have been regicides.'

Then Monsieur Bonnenfant stepped in: 'Tell me then, Monsieur Rade, why it is always the good and not the bad who are attacked. Henri IV, the Great, was assassinated; Louis XV died in his bed. Our King Louis-Philippe was a target for murderers all his life, and they say Czar Alexander was a benevolent man. After all, wasn't he the one who emancipated the serfs?'

Monsieur Rade shrugged his shoulders.

'Hasn't a head of department been killed recently?'

Old Grappe, who every day forgot what had happened the day before, cried out, 'A head of department has been killed?'

The aspiring deputy chief, Monsieur Piston, replied, 'Yes, of course, you know perfectly well, the business of the shellfish.'

But old Grappe had forgotten. 'No, I don't remember.'

Monsieur Rade reminded him of the facts.

'Come on, Daddy Grappe, don't you remember how an office worker, a young man, was acquitted for it? One day he wanted to go out to buy some shellfish for his lunch. His boss refused permission; the lad insisted; the boss told him to be quiet and stay put; the fellow defied him, and picked up his hat; the boss rushed at him, and in the struggle the young fellow plunged his official issue scissors into his boss's chest. A truly bureaucratic ending, don't you agree?'

'There may be something to be said for it,' pronounced Monsieur Bonnenfant. 'There are limits to authority; no section head has the right to organise my dinner and to dictate my appetite. My work belongs to him, but not my stomach. It is an unfortunate case, of course, but there are things to be said for it.'

The aspiring deputy chief, Monsieur Piston, was infuriated and shouted, 'I, monsieur, I say that a section head should be master in his office, like the captain on a ship; authority is indivisible, otherwise official service would be impossible. The authority of the head comes from the government; he represents the State in the office; his absolute right to command is indisputable.'

Monsieur Bonnenfant was getting angry too. Monsieur Rade calmed them down. 'I'll tell you what I'm expecting,' he said. 'One more word and Bonnenfant will plunge his paper knife in Piston's stomach. It's the same with kings. Princes have a way of looking at authority which the people don't share. It's always a matter of shellfish. "I want to eat shellfish, I do!" "No, you can't have any!" "But I want to!" "No!" "I want to!" "No!" And that's enough sometimes to lead to the death of a man or a king.'

But Monsieur Perdrix came back to his idea: 'All the same,' he said, 'the job of a ruler is no fun these days. Really, I like ours the better for it. It's like being a fireman – that's no joke either!'

Monsieur Piston, calmer now, replied, 'French firemen are the pride of the nation.'

Monsieur Rade approved, 'The firemen, yes, but not their equipment.'*

Monsieur Piston defended the equipment and the organisation, and he added, 'Besides, the matter is being looked into; competent men are dealing with it. Before long we will have means commensurate with the need.'

But Monsieur Rade was shaking his head.

---

* This passage is a satirical commentary on a recent event. There had been a serious fire in the department store Le Printemps on 9 March 1881, less than two weeks before this story appeared; twelve people had been injured, and one fireman died.

'Do you believe that? Ah! You do believe it! Well, you are mistaken, monsieur; nothing will change. They don't change systems in France. The American system is to have water, a great deal of water, rivers of it; for shame, how clever to put fires out with oceans of water at hand. In France, on the other hand, it is all left to initiative, intelligence, inventiveness; no water, no pumps, nothing, nothing but the firemen, so the French system amounts to grilling the firemen. Those poor devils, heroes all, put fires out with blows from their axes! How superior to the American way, just think of it! ... Then, when a few of them have been allowed to roast, the Municipal Council speaks, the Colonel speaks, the deputies speak; the two systems are discussed, water versus initiative! And some dignitary or other pronounces over the grave of the victims:

Not goodbye, firemen, but *au revoir* (chorus).

There you are, monsieur, that's how it's done in France.'
Old Grappe, who forgot conversations as soon as they had taken place, asked, 'Where have I heard that verse you just said:

Not goodbye, firemen, but *au revoir.*'

'It's from Beranger,' replied Monsieur Rade gravely.*
Monsieur Bonnenfant, lost in thought, sighed, 'But what a catastrophe, all the same, that Printemps fire!'
Monsieur Rade took him up. 'Now we can talk about it coolly (no pun intended), we have the right I think to take issue to some degree with the eloquence of the director of that establishment. A man with a heart, they say, and I don't doubt it; a skilled

---

* He is pulling the old man's leg. It is not by Beranger, the famous writer of popular songs much derided by Maupassant and Flaubert, but a parody of the speech given by the firemen's colonel over the grave of the man who died in the Printemps fire.

businessman, that's obvious; but an orator, that I deny.'

'Why so?' asked Monsieur Perdrix.

'Because if the fearful disaster which struck him had not at-tracted everyone's sympathy, they wouldn't have been able to laugh enough at La Palisse's speech when he calmed the fears of his employees: "Gentlemen," he more or less said, "you don't know how you are going to eat tomorrow? Nor do I. Oh, look here, you really have to feel sorry for me. Fortunately I have friends. One of them lent me ten centimes to buy a cigar (at times like this you don't smoke a Havana); another put one franc seventy-five at my disposal to take a cab; a third, richer, loaned me twenty-five francs to get a jacket at La Belle Jardinière. Yes I, the director of Le Printemps, I went to La Belle Jardinière! I got fifteen centimes from another person for something else and, since I did not even have an umbrella, I bought an umbrella-sunshade in alpaca for five francs twenty-five, with the help of a fifth loan. Then, my hat itself hav-ing been burned, and as I didn't want to borrow any more, I picked up a fireman's helmet ... look, here it is! Follow my example, if you have friends, throw yourselves on their mercy ... As for myself, you can see, my poor children, that I am up to my neck in debt!"

'But surely one of his employees could have answered: "What does that prove, governor? Three things: One, that you had no money in your pocket. The same happens to me when I forget my wallet, but that does not prove that you have no property or houses, investments or insurance. Two, it further proves that you have credit with your friends; so much the better, use it. Three, it proves finally that you are very unfortunate. Good Lord, we know that, and we are sincerely sorry for you. But that won't improve our situ-ation. You have really landed us in it with your penny bazaar equip-ment, and that's the truth."'

This time everyone in the office was in agreement. Monsieur

Bonnenfant added, jokingly, 'I would have liked to see all the shop girls when they ran out in their petticoats.'

Monsieur Rade went on, 'What's more, I have no confidence in these dormitories for vestal virgins who were nearly roasted to death (like the bus company's horses in their stables last year). If they had to shut something up, it would have been better to put the lamplighters under lock and key, not the poor girls from Lingerie, for goodness' sake!* A director, damn it, cannot be held responsible for all the assets kept under his roof. The clerks' belongings were burned in the cash desk; let's at least hope the young ladies' assets were safe! What I do admire, for instance, is the hunting horn they used to summon the employees. Oh, gentlemen! What a fifth act it would make. You can imagine the big galleries full of smoke, lit up with bright flames, the stampede to escape, everyone terrified – and there, standing erect in the tiered central circle in his slippers and underpants, blowing as hard as he can, is a modern Hernani, a Roland of Haberdashery!'

Monsieur Perdrix, the filing clerk, suddenly announced, 'All the same we are living in a strange century, in a very disturbed period – what about that affair in the Rue Duphot …'

But the office boy abruptly opened the door, 'The boss has arrived, gentlemen.'

Then, in a second, they all fled, slipped away, disappeared, as though the Ministry itself was on fire.

First published in Le Gaulois *on 21 March 1881. This is the first English translation.*

---

* The shop girls lived in dormitories under the roof and were locked in at night. Maupassant is using accurate details and is sharply satirical about the shop director Monsieur Jaluzot, who did borrow two francs fifty to get a cab and made other supremely tactless remarks to the press, causing very caustic comment in the papers.

Recollection

There had been nothing to eat since the day before. Throughout the day we stayed hidden in a barn, huddled up to each other to feel less cold, the officers mixed up with the soldiers, and all of them stupefied with fatigue.

A few sentries, lying down in the snow, were keeping watch on the surroundings of the abandoned farm we were using as a refuge to protect us from surprise attack. They were changed every hour, so they would not become sluggish.

Those of us who were able to sleep were sleeping; the others remained motionless, sitting on the ground, saying a few words to their neighbour from time to time.

For the last three months, like a sea breaking through, the invasion had been coming in everywhere. Great floods of men were arriving one after another, throwing up a scum of looters around them.

As for us, reduced to two hundred *franc-tireurs*[*] from the eight hundred we had been a month before, we were beating a retreat, surrounded by enemies, encircled, lost. Before the next day we had to reach Blainville, where we were still hoping to find General C—. If we did not succeed during the night in covering the twelve leagues which separated us from the town, or else if the French

---

[*] A light corps which is not part of the regular army; there were many such volunteer corps in the Franco-Prussian war. The story is set at the time of the retreat before the advancing Prussian army in December 1870.

division had withdrawn, there would no longer be any hope for us!

Marching was impossible during the day, since the countryside was full of Prussians.

By five o'clock it was night – that pallid sort of night you get when there is snow. The silent white flakes were falling, falling, shrouding everything in a big frozen sheet, growing ever thicker beneath the innumerable hordes and incessant accumulation of nebulous flakes of crystalline cotton wool.

At six o'clock the detachment set out.

Four men went ahead to reconnoitre, alone, three hundred metres forward. Then came a platoon of ten men commanded by a lieutenant, then the rest of the troop, all at once, arranged anyhow, according to the depth of their exhaustion and the length of their stride. At four hundred metres on our flanks, a few soldiers were advancing two by two.

The white dust coming down from the clouds was completely covering us, no longer melting on our caps or greatcoats, turning us into ghosts, like the spectres of dead soldiers.

Sometimes we would rest for a few minutes. Then you heard nothing but the vague swish of falling snow, that almost imperceptible murmur made by the blending of the flakes. A few men were shaking themselves, others were not moving. Then an order went round in a low voice. Guns were shouldered and, wearily, the march began again.

Suddenly the advance guard fell back. Something was making them anxious. The word 'halt' went round. There was a big wood ahead of us. Six men went off to reconnoitre. We waited in gloomy silence.

All at once a piercing cry, a woman's cry, that agonizing and ringing note they use when they're terrified, came through the night air thick with snow.

After a few minutes two prisoners were brought back, an old man and a young girl.

The captain questioned them in a low voice.

'Your name?'

'Pierre Bernard.'

'Your occupation?'

'Butler to Count de Roufé.'

'Is this your daughter?'

'Yes.'

'What does she do?'

'She is linen maid at the château.'

'How do you come to be wandering about like this, at night, for God's sake?'

'We are escaping.'

'Why?'

'Twelve uhlans passed through tonight. They shot three keepers and hanged the gardener. I'm worried for the youngster.'

'Where are you going?'

'To Blainville.'

'Why?'

'Because they say a French army is there.'

'Do you know the way?'

'Certainly.'

'Good enough, stay beside me.'

And the march across the fields began again. The silent old man followed the captain. His daughter was trailing along near him. All at once she stopped.

'Father', she said, 'I'm so tired I can't go any further.'

With that she fell down. She was trembling with cold, and seemed ready to die. Her father wanted to carry her, but he could not even lift her up.

The captain was stamping his feet, swearing, at once furious and moved to pity. 'For God's sake, I can't leave you to croak there!'

A few men had gone off; they came back with cut branches. In a minute a litter was made.

The captain's tone softened: 'My God! That's kind, that is. Come on, boys, who's going to lend his greatcoat? It's for a woman, for God's sake!'

Twenty greatcoats were taken off in a flash and thrown on to the litter. In a second the young girl, wrapped in the soldiers' warm clothes, found herself lifted up by six strong arms and carried off.

We left again as though we had drunk a draught of wine, more bravely, more joyfully. Even a few jokes were cracked, and there was a surge of gaiety such as a woman's presence always produces in a man of French blood.

Now the soldiers were going at a good marching pace, humming tunes, suddenly revived. And an old *franc-tireur*, who was following the litter waiting his turn to replace the first comrade who faltered, poured out his heart to his neighbour. 'I ain't young myself, and bless me! The fair sex, there's nothing like 'em to put a bit of guts in you.'

Until three in the morning we advanced with almost no rest; then, abruptly, like a breath, the order 'Halt!' was whispered once again. Almost instinctively everyone dropped flat on the ground.

Over there, in the middle of the open country, something was moving. It seemed to be running and, since the snow was no longer falling, you could vaguely make out, still very far off, what appeared to be a monster which seemed to lengthen like a snake, then suddenly get smaller, gather itself into a ball, and stretch out once more as it increased speed; over and over it would stop and start off again.

Whispered orders were going round the men as they lay on the ground; from time to time you could hear a sharp little metallic sound.

Suddenly the wandering shape came closer, and we could see galloping up, one behind the other, twelve uhlans lost in the night.

They were so close now that we could hear the horses' breath, the clanking of weapons and the creaking of leather saddles.

Then the captain shouted in his powerful voice, 'Fire, for God's sake!'

Fifty gunshots burst through the icy silence of the fields; four or five late blasts went off, then another, all alone, the last one; and when the blinding effect of the blazing gunpowder had worn off you could see that the twelve men, along with nine horses, had fallen. Three animals were running away at a frantic gallop, and one was trailing behind it the corpse of its rider, hanging by a foot in the stirrup and bouncing about.

The joyful captain cried, 'That's twelve less, by God!' A soldier from the ranks responded, 'That's made a few widows!' Another added, 'Doesn't take long to make that leap, does it?'

Then, from deep in the litter, under the pile of greatcoats, a sleepy little voice emerged: 'What's happening, father? Why is there shooting?' The old man replied, 'It's nothing; go to sleep, little one!' We set off again.

We marched for nearly another four hours.

The sky was getting paler; the snow was becoming bright, luminous, glistening; a cold wind was sweeping away the clouds; and a pale rosiness, like a thin wash of watercolour, was spreading in the east.

A distant voice suddenly cried: 'Who goes there?' Another voice answered. The whole detachment came to a halt. The captain himself went on ahead.

We waited a long time. Then we began to advance. Soon you

could see a farm and, standing in front of it, a French sentry holding a gun. A commanding officer on horseback was watching us go past. All at once he asked, 'What are you carrying on that stretcher?' Then the greatcoats began to move; first you could see two little hands come out, pushing them apart, then a dishevelled head with the hair all snowy but smiling, and it answered, 'It's me, monsieur. I've had a good sleep, believe me. I'm not cold.' A shout of laughter went up from the men, a laugh of lively satisfaction; an enthusiast shouted '*Vive la République!*' to give voice to his joy, and the whole troop, as though suddenly gone mad, frantically bellowed '*Vive la République!*'

Twelve years passed by.

The other day at the theatre the delicate head of a young, blonde woman awoke in me a confused recollection, a haunting recollection, but one I could not pin down. I was soon so bothered by wanting to know the name of this woman that I was asking everyone for it.

Someone said to me, 'She is the Viscountess L—, Count de Roufé's daughter.'

And all the details of that night during the war came flooding into my memory so clearly that straight away, so he could write about it for the public, I told them to my neighbour in the stalls, my friend, who signs himself

Maufrigneuse

'*Souvenir*' *was first published on 16 February 1882 in* Gil Blas. *Maupassant used the pseudonym Maufrigneuse in that paper but wrote under his own name in* Le Gaulois. *The story has not previously been translated into English.*

Other Times

In the last century, when a gentleman gallantly ruined his mistress, he immediately enjoyed an increase in his good reputation. If the mistress, thus denuded, was a great lady and if, abandoned once her purse was empty, she was replaced by another whom the seducer robbed with the same ease and the same appetite, then he would become a *roué*, a man of fashion, highly regarded, envied and respected; people bowed deeply to him, were jealous of him, and he enjoyed all the favours of women and of the powerful.

Alas, alas! A century later, the educated youth of the Latin Quarter, displaying and practising a quite different morality from that of those earlier great lords, and getting carried away by strict principles – these youths fell in a fury on a few souls who have simply remained faithful to the traditions of the past, our great, elegant, aristocratic past, and threw them into the water to see if they could swim.* The supposed victims who got away, the descendants of the roués, are of course poor and miserable, cast out by Providence with no means of support on to the pavements of Paris, although they were born with the instincts of millionaires and their spending needs are poorly served by a native weakness which

---

* The background to this story is a proposed law to make living off women illegal; it caused great press comment. Maupassant refers to the 1882 action of students in the Latin Quarter who turned the ponces (*mackerel* in French, hence the reference to swimming) out of the Jardin du Luxembourg, and one of them was thrown in the fountain. The students were then assaulted by the police since students, as always, were presumed to be rowdy and drunk.

makes them disinclined to work.

Their reasoning, which would seem just if we did not know it to be false, is this: throughout the world there are thousands of women whose sole occupation consists of ruining men by taking advantage of the impure feelings the women themselves inspire in them. Therefore it is simple justice to take back from these same women the money they have obtained by these dishonest means, by inspiring in them in their turn feelings that are no less impure.

This is quite simply a matter of applying the principles of homoeopathic medicine to morals – bad treated by worse. Yet if the homoeopathic method cures! We can draw our own conclusions.

The upshot of the affair was that the avengers of honesty were beaten, imprisoned, flattened, pulverized by the forces of law and order; the men who suffered a drenching were simple, inoffensive bourgeois returning from their offices and going home to their families; those who trade in women, called procurers, can only profit from the free publicity they get; the policemen who did their duty will be dismissed, and the Prefect of Police, for all he can do about it, will no doubt be turned out of office.

So everything is for the best in the best of worlds.

So much for the efficacy of movements in pursuit of a good cause, revolutions, indignation and, in general, all the worthy feelings that inspire men of duty to take action.

They are certainly much wiser in the country. The following scene has been only too faithfully retailed.

I saw it, I tell you, saw it with my own eyes, etc.*

In the Magistrate's Court in Normandy.

The justice of the peace, a fat asthmatic man, sits before a large table, attended by his clerk. He is wearing a grey jacket adorned

---

* The narrator is echoing a line from Molière's *Tartuffe*.

with metal buttons, and he is speaking slowly as he expectorates the air which is whistling in his respiratory tubes as though a leak had been discovered in them.

At the end of the large room there are peasants in blue overalls, sitting on benches, caps or hats between their legs. They are serious, clod-like and wily, and they are running over in their heads the arguments in their cases. They constantly spit beside their feet, which are encased in shoes the size of fishing boats, and a pool of saliva has gathered by each of them.

Opposite the magistrate, just the other side of the table, stand the plaintiffs as their cases are heard.

The plaintiff in the present case is a lady from the country, her face burning with the red blotches of a fifty-year-old beneath a hat that seems to be laden with the produce of her vegetable garden – asparagus, radishes and onions running to seed. She is dry, sharp, horrible and pretentious, she wears knitted gloves and the ribbons in her hair fly about her head like pennants on a ship.

The accused, a big lad of twenty-eight, chubby, inane, looks like an overfed choir boy who has grown too fast. She and he are throwing furious looks at each other.

He is helped and supported by his father, an old peasant closely resembling a rat, and by his young wife, who is red with rage but fresh with it, a big, healthy, pomaded farm girl, reproductive material good enough to win prizes in a show.

The facts are these. The woman, widow of a health officer,* had brought up the youth most carefully and was keeping him for her pleasure. After he had rendered her many services, she had made him a gift of a little farm as a token of her good will. Thus endowed,

---

* In those days, a doctor who was less qualified than one with a doctorate in medicine.

the lad immediately got married, abandoning the old lady, and she, incensed, demanded her property back: the boy or the farm, it was up to him.

The perplexed judge had just heard the woman's complaint. No one laughed. The matter was serious and deserved consideration.

The lad in his turn got up to reply.

The magistrate questioned him.

'What do you have to say?'

'She give me the farm.'

'Why did she give it to you? What have you done to deserve it?'

The lad, outraged, went red to his ears.

'What did I do, my good m'sieur justice of the peace? Look here, it's fifteen years she used me as her fancy man, that poisonous old bag, and she can't say as how it wasn't well worth that!'

This time there was a murmur among the spectators, and convinced voices were repeating, 'Oh, yes, it was well worth that!'

The father thought it a good moment to intervene: 'D'ye think I would've given out the child from the age of fifteen if I hadn't been counting on a decent return?' Then the young woman in her turn came forward vehemently, in irritation, and raised her hand to the red, impassive woman: 'Just look on her, m'sieur judge, look on her. How can you say it wasn't worth that!'

The magistrate considered the old woman at length, consulted with his clerk, concluded that in fact it was well worth that, and dismissed the plaintiff. And everyone present approved the decision.

*Et nunc erudimini.**

'Autre temps' was published in Gil Blas *on 14 June 1882. This is the first English translation.*

---

* 'And be now instructed.' (Psalms II.10: 'Be wise now therefore, O ye kings: be instructed, ye judges of the earth.')

Yveline Samoris

'Countess Samoris.'

'The woman in black, over there?'

'That's the one, she is wearing mourning for her daughter whom she killed.'

'Go on! What kind of a tale are you telling me?'

'Quite a simple story, with no crime and no violence.'

'What it's about, then?'

'Almost nothing. Many courtesans were born to be honest women, so they say, and many women said to be honest were destined to be courtesans, isn't that so? Now Madame Samoris, who was born a courtesan, had a daughter who was born an honest woman, that's all.'

'I don't really understand.'

'I'll explain.'

The Countess Samoris is one of those flashy foreigners, hundreds of whom pour into Paris every year. A Hungarian or a Wallachian countess, or I don't know what, she appeared one winter in an apartment on the Champs-Elysées, the adventurer's quarter, and opened her salon to all comers, anyone and everyone.

I went there. Why? you ask. I don't really know. I went there as we all do, because there is gaming, because the women are easy and the men dishonest. You know this world of swindlers with their assortment of decorations, all noble, all titled, all unknown to their embassies, except for the spies. All of them talk about honour at the drop of a hat, refer to their ancestors, tell their life story – braggarts, liars, cheats, as treacherous as their cards, as deceptive as their names, the aristocracy of the clink, in fact.

I love those people. They are interesting to study, interesting to get to know, amusing to listen to, often witty, never banal like civil servants. Their women are always pretty, with a little touch of foreign roguery and mysterious lives perhaps half spent at reform school. In general they have superb eyes and incredible hair. I love them too.

Madame Samoris is the model for these female adventurers, elegant, mature and still beautiful, a feline enchantress – you can sense that she is vicious to the marrow. It was very entertaining at her place, there was gambling, there was dancing, there was supper … well, everything went on there that makes social life a pleasure.

And she had a daughter, tall, magnificent, always joyful, always ready to celebrate, always laughing wholeheartedly and dancing until she dropped. A real adventuress's daughter. But she was an innocent, ignorant, naive girl, who saw nothing, knew nothing, understood nothing, guessed nothing of what was going on under the parental roof.

'How do you know?'

How do I know? That's the funniest thing of all. My doorbell rang one morning and my valet came to warn me that Monsieur Joseph Bonenthal wanted to speak to me. I said straight away, 'Who is this gentleman?'

My man replied, 'I am not too sure, monsieur, he may be a servant.'

In fact he was a servant, and he wanted to come and work for me.

'What was your last position?'

'I was with the Countess Samoris.'

'Ah! But my house is nothing like hers.'

'I know that very well, monsieur, and that is why I would like to come to monsieur. I have had enough of those people; you pass through, but you don't stay with them.'

As it happened I needed a manservant; I took him on.

A month later Mademoiselle Yveline Samoris died mysteriously, and these are the details of her death as I got them from Joseph, who got them from his friend the Countess's personal maid.

On the evening of a dance two new arrivals were talking behind a door. Mademoiselle Yveline, who had just been dancing, pushed open this door a little to get some air. They did not see her, but she overheard them. They were saying:

'But who is the young person's father?'

'A Russian, apparently, Count Rouvaloff. He doesn't see her mother any more.'

'And who's today's ruling prince?'

'That English prince standing in front of the window. Madame Samoris adores him – but her adoration never lasts more than a month to six weeks. Besides you can see that she has a numerous company of friends; all are called … and almost all are chosen. It's a bit expensive but … worth it!'

'Where did she get the name Samoris?'

'From perhaps the only man she loved, an Israelite banker from Berlin called Samuel Morris.'

'Good. Thank you. Now you've filled me in I can see clearly how the land lies. And I'll go straight for it.'

What storm burst in the brain of that young girl, endowed as she was with all the instincts of an honest woman? What despair deranged that simple mind? What tortures dimmed that perpetual happiness, that charming laugh, that exultant *joie de vivre?* What battle raged in the young girl's heart until the last guest had left? That, of course, Joseph was not able to tell me. But that very evening Yveline abruptly entered her mother's bedroom as she was about to get into bed, dismissed the maid (who lingered behind the door) and, large-eyed, pale, standing upright, she announced:

'Mother, this is what I heard just now in the salon.'

And word for word she repeated the remarks I have told you.

The amazed countess did not know what to answer at first. Then she energetically denied everything, invented a story, swore, called God as her witness.

The young girl withdrew, distraught but not convinced. And she began to spy.

I can remember perfectly well the strange change she went through. She was always serious and sad and fixed her big eyes upon us as though she wanted to read the depths of our souls. We didn't know what to make of it, and someone said she was looking for a husband, either permanent or temporary.

One evening she was left in no doubt; she caught her mother. Then, coldly, like a businessman setting out the conditions of an agreement, she said, 'Mother, this is what I have decided. We will both retire to a small town, or else to the country; we will live there quietly, as best we can. Your jewels alone are worth a fortune. If you manage to marry some honest man, so much the better; even better if I do as well. If you don't agree, I will kill myself.'

This time the countess sent her daughter to bed and forbade her ever again to utter such a speech, which was unseemly coming from her.

Yveline replied, 'I will give you a month to think about it. If in a month our life has not changed I will kill myself, because there is no other honourable way out for me.'

And she left.

A month later they were still dancing and taking late suppers at the Samoris house.

Yveline claimed she had toothache and had a few drops of chloroform bought from a pharmacy near by. The next day she did the same; and every day she went out and must have collected tiny doses of the narcotic herself. She filled a bottle full of it.

They found her one morning in her bed, already cold, with a cotton mask over her face.

Her coffin was covered in flowers, the church was hung with white. There was a crowd at the funeral.

In all honesty, if I had known – but you never do know – maybe I would have married that girl. She was awfully pretty.

'And the mother, what became of her?'

'Oh, she cried a great deal. She only began to receive her closest friends again a week ago.'

'And how did they explain the death?'

'They talked of a new make of stove that had malfunctioned. There was a great to-do a while back about accidents with those appliances, so it wasn't hard to believe.'

'Yveline Samoris' was first published on 20 December 1882 in Le Gaulois. *It has never before been translated into English.*

The Cough

For Armand Silvestre *

My dear friend and colleague,

I have a little story for you, an innocuous little story. If I manage to tell it well, as well as she who told it to me, I hope you will like it.

The task is not at all an easy one, for my friend is a woman of infinite wit, free in her speech. I don't have the same resources. I am not able, as she is, to give that crazy gaiety to the things I relate; and, reduced to the necessity of not using words that are too specific, I declare myself impotent to find, as you do, delicate equivalents.

My friend, who besides is a very talented woman in the theatre world, has not authorised me to make her story public.

So I am at pains to preserve her copyright in case she wishes, one day or another, to write about this adventure herself. She would do it better than me, I don't doubt. Being a greater expert on the subject, she would discover a thousand amusing details as well, which I cannot invent.

But look at the embarrassment I am falling into. From the first word I am going to have to find an equivalent term, and I would like it to be an inspired one. 'The Cough' is not my sort of thing. In order to be understood I need annotations at least, or a paraphrase in the style of the Abbé Delille:

---

* Armand Silvestre was a friend and colleague of Maupassant's on the newspaper *Gil Blas*. Though best known for his stories of scatological, Rabelaisian humour, he was one of the Parnassian poets and was also an art critic.

The cough which concerns us does not come from the throat.

She was sleeping (my friend) beside a man she loved. It was at night, naturally.

She was not very familiar with this man, or at least had not been so for long. These things happen sometimes, mostly among theatre people. Bourgeois women may well be amazed. As for sleeping beside a man it doesn't matter whether you know him very well or little, it hardly affects what goes on in the privacy of the bed. If I were a woman, I think I would prefer new friends; they must be more agreeable, in every way, than the *habitués*.

In what is called polite society, there is a different way of looking at things, which is not mine. I am sorry for it on behalf of the women of that world; but I wonder if the way of looking at things much affects the way of going about them? …

So she was sleeping beside a new friend. That is an excessively difficult and delicate affair. With an old companion you can be at ease, you are not embarrassed, you can turn over when you like, give a few kicks, invade three-quarters of the mattress, pull at all the blankets and roll yourself in them, snore, grunt, cough (I'm saying cough for lack of an alternative) or sneeze. (What do you make of sneeze as a synonym?)

But to get to that stage you need at least six months of intimacy, and I'm talking about people who are open by nature. The rest always maintain a certain reserve, which for my part I approve. But perhaps we don't have the same feelings on this subject.

When it is a matter of a new acquaintance whom one may suppose to be feeling sentimental, you certainly have to make a little effort not to inconvenience the person who shares your bed and to try to keep up a certain poetic magic and a certain control.

She was sleeping. But suddenly she felt a discomfort, interior, piercing, mobile. It began in the pit of the stomach and began to rumble as it descended towards … towards … towards the lower throat regions with the discreet noise of intestinal thunder.

The man, the new friend, was stretched out peacefully, on his back, eyes closed. She looked at him sideways, anxious, hesitant.

Colleague, have you ever been at a first night with a chesty cold? The whole audience is attentive, breathing in total silence; but you are no longer hearing anything, you are waiting desperately for a moment of disturbance so that you can cough. Along the whole length of your gullet you experience terrible ticklings and pricklings. Finally you can hang on no longer. Hard luck on your neighbours. You cough – The whole theatre cries, 'Outside.'

She was in the same state, ravaged, tortured by a mad desire to cough. (When I say cough, of course I mean you to transpose.)

He seemed to be sleeping; he was breathing calmly. He was certainly asleep.

She said to herself, 'I will be careful. I will try just to blow, gently, so as not to wake him.' And she made as though to cover her mouth with her hand and to clear her throat, silently, by letting out the air in a controlled fashion.

Maybe she did it badly, maybe the irritation was too great, but she coughed.

At once she lost her head. If he had heard, how shameful! And how dangerous! Oh! if by chance he was not asleep? How could she find out? She looked at him fixedly and, by the glow of the nightlight, she thought she saw a smile on the face with its eyes closed. But if he was laughing … then he was not asleep … and if he wasn't asleep …?

With her mouth, the real one, she tried to make a similar noise to … put her companion off.

It bore no resemblance.

But was he asleep?

She turned over, fidgeted, pushed him, so she could be sure.

He didn't move.

So she began to hum softly.

The gentleman did not move.

Losing her head, she called him, 'Ernest.'

He didn't make a movement, but he replied at once, 'What do you want?'

Her heart lurched. He was not asleep; he had never been asleep! ...

She asked, 'Aren't you asleep, then?'

He murmured resignedly, 'You can see I'm not.'

Appalled, she didn't know what to say any more. At last she replied, 'Did you hear anything?'

He answered, still motionless, 'No.'

She felt a wild desire to hit him coming over her, and, sitting up in bed, 'Yet I thought ...?'

'What?'

'That someone was moving about in the house.'

He smiled. Certainly this time she had seen him smile, and he said, 'Leave me alone, you've been bothering me for half an hour now.'

She quivered.

'Me? ... That's a bit much. I've only just woken up. You heard nothing then?'

'Yes, I did.'

'Ah! At last, you heard something! What?'

'Someone ... coughed!'

She leapt up and cried out, exasperated, 'Someone coughed! Where? Who coughed? Are you mad? Answer me then!'

He began to lose patience.

'Come on, that's enough of that old tale. You know quite well it was you.'

This time she was furious, shouting, 'Me? Me? Me? I coughed? Me? I coughed! Oh! it's an insult, it's an outrage, it's contemptible. Well, goodbye! I won't stay with a man who treats me like that.'

And she started to jump out of the bed.

He replied in a weary voice, wanting peace at any price, 'Look, calm down. It was me who coughed.'

But she burst out angrily once more: 'What? You ... coughed in my bed! ... Beside me ... while I was sleeping? And you admit it. You are despicable. And you think I'm going to stay with a man who ... coughs next to me. Who do you take me for?'

With that she stood right up on the bed, trying to climb over him to get away.

He calmly took her by the feet and made her lie down beside him, and laughed, lightly and mockingly. 'Look, Rose, calm down, will you. You coughed. Because it was you. I'm not complaining, I'm not annoyed; I even like it. But, Good Lord, come to bed.'

This time she escaped with a jump and leaped into the room; and as she desperately searched for her clothes, she repeated, 'You think I'm going to stay with a man who allows a woman to ... cough in his bed. My dear, you are despicable.'

So he got up, and first he slapped her. Then, since she fought back, he beat her all over; then, picking her up in his arms, he threw her full length on to the bed.

She remained stretched out, inert and crying against the wall, so he got in next to her, then, turning his back to her as well, he coughed ... he had fits of coughing ... with silences and with encores. From time to time he asked, 'Have you had enough?'

and, as she didn't reply, he would begin again.

All at once she began to laugh, but like a madwoman, crying, 'How funny he is, oh! How funny he is!'

And she suddenly took him in her arms, fastening her mouth to his, murmuring between her lips, 'I love you, *mon chat.*'

And they didn't sleep any more ... until the morning.

That is my story, my dear Silvestre. Forgive this incursion into your domain. There is another euphemism. 'Domain' is not the right word. You amuse me so often that I couldn't resist taking a little risk and coming up in your rear.

But yours is the glory for laying that route wide, wide open.

'La Toux' was first published on 28 January 1883 in Panurge. *It has never before been translated into English.*

The Avenger

When Antoine Leuillet married the widow Madame Mathilde Souris he had been in love with her for almost ten years.

Monsieur Souris had been his friend, his old school fellow. Leuillet liked him very much but found him a bit of a muggins. He would often say, 'That poor Souris won't set the world on fire.'

When Souris married Mademoiselle Mathilde Duval, Leuillet was surprised and a bit put out, as he had taken quite a fancy to her. She was the daughter of a neighbour, a former draper who had retired on her very small capital. She was pretty, sharp, intelligent. She took Souris for his money.

Then Leuillet's hopes took a different turn. He courted his friend's wife. He was good looking, not stupid, rich too. He believed he was sure to succeed; he failed. Then he fell thoroughly in love and became the kind of lover whose close friendship with the husband makes him discreet, timid, embarrassed. Madame Souris thought he had ceased to harbour ambitions about her, and willingly became his friend. That lasted nine years.

Then one morning a messenger brought Leuillet a distraught note from the poor woman. Souris had just died suddenly of an aneurysm.

He had a dreadful shock, for they were the same age, but almost at once a feeling of profound joy, of infinite relief, of release, suffused him body and soul. Madame Souris was free.

All the same he knew how to put on the necessary show of affliction; he waited the right amount of time and respected all the conventions. At the end of fifteen months he married the widow.

This deed was judged to be natural and even generous. It was the act of a friend and a gentleman.

At last he was happy, completely happy.

They lived in the most cordial intimacy, having understood and liked each other from the start. They kept no secrets from each other and told each other their most intimate thoughts. Leuillet loved his wife now with a peaceful and assured love, he loved her as a tender and devoted companion who was his equal and his confidante. But in his mind there remained a strange and inexplicable rancour against the late Souris, who had possessed this woman first, who had had the flower of her youth and of her mind, who had even taken a little of the poetry out of her. The memory of the dead husband was spoiling the happiness of the living husband; and this posthumous jealousy was now tearing at Leuillet's heart night and day. It made him talk incessantly of Souris, to ask for a thousand intimate and secret details about him, to want to know everything about his person and his habits. And he pursued him to his very grave with mockery, complacently recalling his failings, stressing his absurdities, dwelling on his deficiencies.

He would constantly call his wife, from one end of the house to the other:

'Hey, Mathilde?'

'Here, my love.'

'Come and talk to me.'

She would arrive, always smiling, knowing quite well they

were going to talk about Souris and indulging this harmless idiosyncrasy in her new husband.

'I say, do you remember one day when Souris wanted to prove to me that small men are always more loved than tall ones?'

And he would launch into some unpleasant reflection upon the departed, who was small, and discreetly to his own, Leuillet's, advantage, who was tall.

Madame Leuillet would give him to understand that he was quite right, quite right; and she laughed in all sincerity, gently mocking her former spouse for the greater pleasure of the new one, who always ended by adding: 'All the same, that Souris, what a muggins he was.'

They were happy, completely happy. Leuillet never ceased proving his unassuaged love to his wife in all the usual ways.

However, one night as they lay awake, both of them aroused by a renewal of youth, Leuillet, who was clasping his companion tightly in his arms and kissing her deeply, asked her all of a sudden:

'Darling, tell me ...'

'Mm'm?'

'Souris ... this is hard to say, what I'm going to ask you ... Souris, was he very ... very loving?'

She gave him a big kiss and murmured, 'Not as much as you, my pet.'

His masculine pride was flattered and he went on, 'He must have been ... a muggins ... was he?'

She did not answer. She only gave a little mischievous laugh as she hid her face in her husband's neck.

He asked: 'He must have been a real muggins, and not ... not ... how can I put it ... not skilful?'

She gave a slight movement of her head as if to say, 'No ... not at all skilful.'

He went on, 'He must have annoyed you a lot at night, didn't he?'

This time she yielded to an outburst of frankness and replied, 'Oh! Yes!'

He kissed her once more for these words and whispered, 'What a brute he was! You weren't happy with him?'

She answered, 'No. It wasn't much fun, day after day.'

Leuillet felt charmed, drawing in his mind a comparison entirely to his advantage between his wife's former situation and the present.

For a little while he remained silent, then he had a fit of laughing and asked: 'Look, tell me.'

'What?'

'Will you be quite candid, quite candid with me?'

'Of course, my love.'

'Well, then, seriously, were you never tempted to ... to ... to deceive him, that fool Souris?'

Madame Leuillet gave a little 'Oh!' of modesty and hid herself even more deeply in her husband's chest. But he noticed that she was laughing.

He pressed her: 'Then, truly, do you admit it? He really looked like a deceived husband, that beast! It would be so funny, so funny! Good old Souris. Look, look here, my darling, you could surely admit that, to me, to me especially.'

He emphasised 'to me', naturally thinking that if she had had any inclination to deceive Souris, it was with him, Leuillet, that she would have done it; and he quivered with pleasure as he waited for her to admit it, sure that he would have won her then, had she not been the virtuous woman she was.

119

But she was not answering, and still laughing as though at the recollection of something infinitely comical.

Leuillet, in his turn, began to laugh at the thought that he could have made Souris wear horns! What a fine trick! What a great joke! Ah, yes, a really good joke!

He was spluttering, quite shaken with delight: 'Poor Souris, poor old Souris. Oh, yes, he had the look of one; oh, yes, oh, yes!'

Now Madame Leuillet was twisting about under the sheets, crying until she laughed, almost screaming.

And Leuillet was repeating, 'Go on, confess it, confess it. Be frank. You know quite well it won't be unwelcome to me, not to me.'

Then she faltered, as she was choking: 'Yes, yes.'

Her husband pressed her, 'Yes, what? Go on, tell everything.'

She was no longer laughing except in a discreet way and, raising her lips to Leuillet's ear which awaited a pleasant confidence, she whispered: 'Yes ... I deceived him.'

He felt an icy shiver run right into his bones, and mumbled, dumbfounded: 'You ... you ... deceived him ... completely?'

She still believed he was finding the thing infinitely amusing and replied, 'Yes ... completely ... completely.'

He needed to sit up in bed, he felt so stricken, winded, bowled over as though he had just discovered that it was he himself who wore the horns.

At first he said nothing; then, after a few seconds, he uttered simply: 'Ah!'

She also had stopped laughing, realizing her mistake too late.

At last, Leuillet asked, 'And who with?'

She remained silent, trying to make up a convincing answer.

He went on, 'Who with?'

She said at last, 'With a young man.'

He turned towards her abruptly and said in a cutting voice, 'Of course I didn't think it was with a cook. I am asking you which young man, do you hear?'

She made no reply. He seized the sheet which she had over her head and threw it in the middle of the bed, repeating, 'I want to know with which young man, do you hear?'

Then she said faintly: 'I meant it as a joke.'

But he was shaking with anger. 'What? What did you say? You meant it as a joke? So you were making fun of me? I won't put up with feeble excuses like that, do you hear? I am asking you the young man's name.'

She did not answer, remaining on her back, motionless.

He took her by the arm and shook her vigorously: 'Do you hear me? I expect you to answer me when I speak to you.'

Then she nervously whispered: 'I think you are going mad. Leave me alone!'

He was trembling with rage, no longer knowing what to say, fuming, and he was shaking her with all his strength, repeating, 'Do you hear? Do you hear?'

She made a sudden movement to escape and caught her husband's nose with the end of her fingers. He got in a fury thinking she had hit him and flung himself upon her.

Now he was holding her beneath him, hitting her with all his strength and shouting, 'Take that, and that, and that, there, there, there, slut, whore, whore!'

When he was out of breath, his energy spent, he got up and went to the chest of drawers to make himself a drink sweetened with orange flower water, for he was feeling shattered and faint.

She was crying deep in the bed, heaving great sobs, feeling that all her happiness had come to an end through her own fault.

121

Then, in the midst of her tears, she stammered, 'Listen, Antoine, come here, I lied to you, you'll understand, listen.'

Ready with a defence now, armed with reasoning and cunning wiles, she slightly raised her dishevelled head with its nightcap all askew.

He turned towards her and came closer, ashamed of having beaten her but feeling, alive in his husband's heart, an inextinguishable hatred for this woman who had deceived the other man, Souris.

'Le Vengeur' was first published on 6 November 1883 in Gil Blas. *It has previously been translated into English only in the Artinian edition.*

A True-Life Drama

*Le vrai peut quelquefois n'être pas vraisemblable.**

I was saying the other day in this column that in its novels yesterday's literary school made use of exceptional adventures or truths encountered in real life; while the present school, concerned only with credibility, produces a sort of average of ordinary events.

And now it transpires that I am told a whole story, which apparently happened and which seems as though it has been invented by some popular novelist or crazy dramatist.

In any event, it is gripping, well turned and extremely interesting in its strangeness.

In a country property, half farm and half manor house, there lived a family possessed of a daughter who was courted by two young men, two brothers.

They came of an old and good family and lived together in a neighbouring property.

It was the elder who found favour. The younger brother, his heart distraught with violent passion, became morose, dreamy, wandering. He would go out for whole days, or else he would shut himself in his room and read or meditate.

The closer the time of the marriage approached, the stormier his behaviour was becoming.

About a week before the appointed date the fiancé, who was

---

* Boileau. What is true is sometimes not credible. Or: Truth is stranger than fiction.

123

returning one evening from his daily visit to the young girl, was shot at point-blank range as he passed the edge of a wood. Some farm workers, who found him at dawn, brought the body to his house. His brother plunged into a moody despair which lasted two years. It was even thought he would go into the priesthood or that he would kill himself.

At the end of these two years of despair, he married his brother's fiancée.

However, the murderer had not been found. There was no definite clue; and the only thing that shed any light on the matter was a piece of paper, almost burnt, black with powder, that had been used to ram the murderer's gun. A few lines of verse were printed on this scrap of paper, the end of a song perhaps, but the book from which this leaf had been torn could not be found.

A notorious poacher was suspected of the murder. He was charged, imprisoned, questioned, harassed; but he did not confess, and he was acquitted for lack of proof.

Such are the facts of this drama. You would think you were reading a horrifying adventure story. It has everything: the love of the two brothers, the jealousy of one, the death of the favourite, the crime at the edge of a wood, justice baffled, the accused acquitted, and the slight clue left in the hands of the magistrates, this bit of paper black with powder.

Twenty years passed. The younger brother, married, is happy, rich and respected; he has three daughters. One of them is going to get married in her turn. She is marrying the son of a former magistrate, who had in fact been on the bench at the time of the elder brother's murder.

And here we are with the marriage taking place, a big country wedding, a party. The two fathers are shaking hands, the young people are happy. There is dinner in the long gallery of the manor house; there is drinking, jokes, laughter and, over dessert, someone suggests singing songs, as they used to do in the olden days.

The idea appealed, and everyone sang.

When his turn came, the bride's father racked his brains for the old verses he used to sing, and little by little he remembered them.

He made people laugh, and they clapped; he continued, and sang his last song; then, when he had finished, his neighbour the magistrate asked him: 'Where the devil did you find that song? I recognise the last lines of it. It even seems to be connected with some serious incident in my life, but I don't quite know what; I'm losing my memory a bit.'

The next day the newly married couple left on their honeymoon.

However, the young man's father was harassed by an obsession with dim recollections, that constant itch to find something which continually escapes you. He would incessantly hum the refrain which his friend had sung, and still he could not pin down where those lines came from, yet he felt they had long ago been imprinted in his mind, as though it was seriously in his interest not to forget them.

Two more years passed by. And then one day, leafing through some old papers, he found the rhymes he had looked for so hard, copied out by himself.

They were the lines which had remained legible on the plug of the gun which had been used for the murder years before.

Then he began the investigation again on his own. He asked some shrewd questions, and he searched his friend's furniture, so much and so well that he found the book from which the sheet had been torn.

Now it was in his own heart, the heart of a father, that the drama unfolded. His son was the son-in-law of the man he so strongly suspected; but, if this man was guilty, he had killed his brother to steal his fiancée from him! Could there be a more monstrous crime?

The magistrate got the better of the father. The case was retried. The real murderer was indeed the brother. He was found guilty.

Those are the facts as they were conveyed to me. They are said to be true. Would we be able to use them in a book without appearing to be making a servile imitation of Messieurs de Montepin and Du Boisgobey?*

So, in literature as in life, the axiom 'Not every truth is suitable for telling' seems to me to be perfectly apt. This story seems to afford striking support. A novel written with a subject like that would leave all its readers unconvinced and would disgust all real artists.

'Un drame vrai' was first published in Le Gaulois *on 6 August 1882. It has not previously been translated into English.*

---

* Two popular and prolific writers of the time, now entirely forgotten.

Advice Given in Vain

My dear friend,

The advice you are asking me for is very difficult to give. You tell me you are involved in a liaison that you cannot end, and that seems to me a dreadful position to be in. I am old, you have been told I have led a full life, and you are looking to my experience to help you. I am afraid I may not be able to do anything for you, since you seem to be in a hole.

If I have properly understood your letter, this is your situation. You have become involved with a married woman, who is too clinging. I shall spell things out to be sure I am not making a mistake.

You are young, very young, twenty-five years old. Having put yourself about a bit, to right and left, in the streets and with the women of the street, you felt tempted, as we all are, by a desire for more elegant love affairs.

Then you noticed a friend of your mother's who, on her side, had already been noticing you for some time.

She was just at the age when a woman is still looking good but is on the point of becoming past it. Over forty, carrying a bit of weight, fresh – that freshness of preserved grapes – and with affection to spare, since her husband had not drawn upon those reserves for a long time.

First of all you exchanged looks. Then your handshakes became rather prolonged, closer, with tentative pressure at first, then with meaning. Then, one evening, you kissed her behind a door, and she returned your kiss with interest.

You went out for a walk, delighted, light-hearted, delirious. You were hooked. A few days later the chain was welded. A fearful chain, my poor friend.

First of all your mistress's age alone constitutes a terrible danger. Women, at that point, are looking for their last prey, the bread to put on the table for their old age. They make you comfortable. Well and good, but what difference does that make? An old fox is wilier than a young one. And you must remember that the thing a woman is least willing to give up is love. She puts off the moment of abdication as long as possible and, if possible, right up until she's paralysed with senility. As for me, I would like to see the debauchery of old women punishable by the law, like the corruption of minors. Is it more blameworthy, in fact, to start too soon than to finish too late? In both cases there is a violation of nature.

My poor boy, how sorry I am for you! This business has been going on for five years now, hasn't it? Yes, I know, she was still attractive then. She is not so any longer. Five years at the age when everything is collapsing counts as fifty. You have watched her deteriorate from day to day. When you first took a helping, you had before you an edible dish. Now there are only leftovers … which should be thrown out.

From now on, I am afraid, your only consolation will be to watch her getting older. That at least is a kind of vengeance, and a good one.

I don't see how you will be able to get rid of her, unless you tell your mother, which would not be tactful. She comes to dinner with you twice a week; in the evening she comes at any time. Her husband adores you and takes you to the theatre. That fits the pattern. As for her, she is killing you with kindness, attention, affection, the unquestionable signs of love.

You know, there are two things which should be taught to

children along with the alphabet:

You should never take a mistress who can no longer be unfaithful to you.

You should be careful, as far as you can be, of liaisons that cannot be undone with money.

When a woman is still desirable you can often get rid of her, with a little skill, at a friend's expense. But you have no hope of that. Still, you want to break it off at any price. Breaking it off! What a problem!

If anybody could write a good manual on the art of breaking it off they would be rendering a greater service to humanity, to men especially, than the inventor of the railways. Let's be practical.

If we were living in another century and in accordance with other customs, I would simply advise you to poison her, because she often comes to dinner. But you would make a mess of it and get caught.

I know perfectly well that there are other ways of poisoning a woman which the law cannot provide for and does not punish. It's not my business to reveal them to you, so let's skip that.

In reality there is really only one good method of breaking up with your mistress: the duck-dive. You disappear and you do not reappear. She writes to you; there is no reply. She comes to see you; you have moved. She looks for you everywhere; you remain unfindable. If by accident you meet her, you pretend not to recognize her, and you pass by. If she stops you, you ask her politely, 'What can I do for you, madam?' And you delight in her amazement, her indignant fury. If you go about things in this way you have nothing to fear but vitriol.* The method has the advantage of being crude and

---

* A frequent method of (mostly feminine) vengeance at the time Maupassant was writing was to throw vitriol (sulphuric acid) in the face of the person abandoning you.

radical. But you could hardly use it in your situation, unfortunately, since you live with your family. The hunted rabbit must always return to its hole; you always have to go back to the family home eventually, however long you stay away. She would catch you when you returned, and that's that.

What to do, then? Face it! You must keep her. I know quite well that now you hate her as much as she disgusts you. Too bad. I feel you'll just have to apply your skill to avoiding openings. Get away, faint, feign attacks of nerves, rabies or epilepsy, shout 'Fire! Murder!' as soon as you are alone; leave your coat somewhere, or more than that; pay a servant to knock on the door as soon as she finds herself alone with you. But accept that you'll have to submit, at least platonically, to her passion.

Now if you absolutely must separate, get yourself caught *in flagrante delicto* by her husband. You'll be free of her at the cost of two months' captivity. That's not much. And don't think this way of handling the matter indelicate – it is as permissible as it is legal.

I am well aware that her husband may not want to surprise you, and you would be exposing yourself to a momentous and very distressing rendezvous. But here's how to draw the suspicious and careful husband into your trap. Write him a love letter and sign it with the name of a pretty young actress asking him for an hour alone together.

All men have a tendency to believe they are irresistible. He will go. You will have told him to enter a particular house without ringing. You will not bolt the door, and you will play for time as long as possible. Whether he is angry or he forgives you, he will get you off the hook. Be careful all the same to have a few witnesses in a wardrobe in case he refuses to acknowledge what he has seen.

Love, my boy, is very nice and very disagreeable at the same time. 'When it is drawn, you must drink it,' as the Marshal of

Saxony said; unfortunately the old wines of affection are not as good as the old wines in the cellar.

I notice that I've given you a long lecture, and I haven't in fact come up with a practical solution. There aren't any. It all depends on your personal skill, on your flexibility and on the people concerned.

How about becoming a priest? Or blowing your brains out?

Or else there remains … marriage! But that would really be going from bad to worse, wouldn't it? And in any case, would it get you out of it?

Finally, just between ourselves, do you know what I would do in your place? It's a mean trick, what I am going to say, but all's fair in self-defence. Well, I would try to make a mother of her, if it's not too late for that. She would dislike you for it so much that she might well leave you.

I would like to see special teaching in schools to prepare young pupils for dangers of this kind. You learn Greek and Latin, which are hardly any use to you, yet they don't teach you to defend yourself against women, who are, after all, the biggest danger in our lives. We should be instructed in their nature, their tricks, their tenacity and a thousand other things. We should be put on our guard against them.

Of course, that might not do any good.

I shake your hand, as one does at the cemetery gate with people one can neither relieve nor console.

Certified as a true copy:

Maufrigneuse

'Vains Conseils' was first published on 26 February 1884 in Gil Blas. This is the first English translation.

Doctors and Patients

What a strange mystery is recollection! You are on your way through the streets in the first sunshine in May, and all at once, as though long-closed doors in the memory were opening, forgotten things come back to you. They pass and are followed by others, making you relive hours past, long past.

Why these sudden returns to times gone by? Who knows? A floating smell, a sensation so slight that you did not notice it but it was registered by one of our sense organs, the eye struck by the same effect of the sun, a noise perhaps, a frisson, a nothing that skimmed over us in earlier circumstances and then encountered again – this is enough to make us suddenly visualize a place, events, people that had vanished from our thoughts.

Why does a breath of air laden with the odours of leaves under the chestnut trees on the Champs-Elysées suddenly evoke a road, a main road, alongside a mountain in the Auvergne?

To the left, between two peaks, appears the heavy and majestic cone of the Puy de Dôme. Around this heavy giant, further off or nearer, rises a host of other peaks. Many of them, which once spat out flames and smoke, seem truncated – dead volcanoes – and their dead craters have become lakes.

To the right the road overlooks an endless plain, populated with towns and villages, rich and wooded: the Limagne. The higher you go the further you can see, as far as other distant summits, the Forez mountains. All this immense horizon is veiled in a soft, clear, silky mist. The far distance in the

Auvergne is infinitely graceful in its transparent haze.

The road is lined with enormous walnut trees which almost always shade it from the sun. The mountain slopes are covered with flowering chestnut trees; the clusters of blossom are paler than the leaves and look grey against the dark green.

From time to time, a ruined manor appears on a mountain top. The countryside is bristling with fortified houses, which are all much the same, however.

Above a vast, square building, festooned with battlements, rises a tower. The walls have no windows, nothing but almost invisible holes. You would think these fortresses had grown on the slopes like mountain mushrooms. They are made of grey stone which is nothing other than lava.

Along all the paths you meet cows in harness pulling domes of hay. The pairs of beasts keep up a slow pace on the steep inclines and falls, pulling or holding back the enormous load. A man walks in front and regulates their pace with a long stick, touching them with it at times. He never hits them. He seems, above all, to guide them with the movements of his rod, like the conductor of an orchestra. He makes measured gestures as he commands his animals, and often turns around to communicate his wishes. You never see horses, except for diligences or hired vehicles, and when it is hot the dust on the roads flies about on gusts of wind, carrying with it a sweet smell slightly redolent of vanilla that makes you think of stables.

The whole countryside is perfumed with scented trees. The vines, their flowers scarcely over, exhale a sweet and exquisite smell. The chestnut trees, the acacias, the limes, the pines, the hay and the wild flowers in the ditches load the air with light and persistent perfume.

The Auvergne is a region of patients. The extinct volcanoes are

133

like closed-up stoves in which mineral waters of every kind are continually being heated in the belly of the earth. From these great hidden casseroles come the hot springs which, according to doctors who have an interest in the matter, contain all the medicines necessary to cure any ailment.

In every spa, founded around every warm spring that a farmer discovers, a whole series of wonderful scenes is enacted. First of all there is the sale of the land by the countryman, then a company (a sham one) is formed with the nominal capital of a few million francs; there follows the miraculous construction of the enterprise with these imaginary funds, and with real stones, the installation of the first doctor, who bears the title of Medical Officer; the first patient appears, and then is performed the eternal, sublime comedy of patient and doctor.

To the observer, every spa town is a California of comedy. The doctors come in a variety of marvellous types, from the very correct physician *à l'anglaise*, complete with white tie, down to the sceptical, artful and witty doctor who regales his friends with the methods and tricks of his trade.

Between these two varieties you find the paternal and good-natured doctor, the scientific doctor, the brutal doctor, the woman's doctor, the doctor with long hair, the elegant doctor and many others. Each variety of doctor infallibly finds the corresponding variety of patient, his naive clientele. And between them, every day, in every hotel room begins anew the wonderful farce, which Molière did not describe in its entirety. Oh, if only these doctors would talk, what notes, what marvellous observations they could share on the nature of man!

Sometimes, mind you – one in a thousand – after a few drinks they do relate some of their adventures.

One of them, a very witty man, had the inspired idea of

announcing in the papers that the waters of B——, which he himself had discovered, prolonged human life. Moreover, there was
no mystery about how they did it. He explained it scientifically
in terms of the action on the organism of salts, minerals and
gases.

He had even written a large pamphlet on the subject, which
also gave details of excursions in the surrounding area.

But he needed proof of his claims. So he went on a little trip
in search of centenarians.

He got them mostly from poor families, who were not keen on
feeding their useless old relatives and would let him have them
for six months in the year; and he installed them in an elegant
villa which he called the 'Centenarian Hospice'. They were not
all a hundred, but they were getting close. They was his advertisement, and a sublime advertisement they were too. Curing is
nothing, but staying alive is everything. His waters didn't cure
them, they made them live! What did it matter about the liver,
the bronchi, the larynx, the kidneys, the stomach, the intestines!
What counted was to stay alive.

Now one day, feeling light-hearted, this great man told the following story.

One morning he was called to a new traveller, Monsieur D——,
who had arrived the previous night and who had rented a house
quite close to the Souveraine spring. He was a little old man of
eighty-six, still spry, lean, healthy and active, and he took infinite care to conceal his age.

He offered the doctor a seat and at once began to interview
him:

'Doctor, if I am well it's thanks to healthy living. Though I am
not of course very old, I am already of a good age, but I avoid all
illnesses and indispositions, even the slightest feelings of being

135

unwell, through healthy living. You say that the climate in this area is conducive to good health; I am quite ready to believe it, but before I settle here I would like proof. So I want you to come to me once a week and give me the following very precise information:

'First of all, I would like a complete and exhaustive list of all the inhabitants of the spa and its environs who are over eighty years old. I would also like a few physical and physiological details about them. I want to know their profession, their way of life, their habits. Every time one of these persons dies, please be so kind as to let me know, giving me the precise cause of death and all the circumstances.'

Then he added graciously, 'I hope, doctor, that we will be good friends,' and he held out his little, wrinkled hand which the doctor shook as he promised his devoted assistance.

The day he was given the list of the seventeen inhabitants of the area who were over eighty, Monsieur D— began to show the greatest interest and infinite solicitude for these old people, whom he was going to watch go down one after another.

He did not want to know them, no doubt because he feared he might discover some resemblance between himself and somebody who might soon die, which would have upset him; but he got a very clear idea of what they were like, and he talked about nothing else with the doctor, who dined with him every Thursday.

He would ask, 'Well, doctor, how is Poinçot today? We left him a little unwell last week.' And when the doctor had given a health report on the patient, Monsieur D— would suggest modifications to his diet, experiments, methods of treatment which he could apply to himself afterwards if they were successful on the others. They were a testing ground, these seventeen old people, which he found instructive.

One evening the doctor announced, as he entered, 'Rosalie Tourul is dead.'

Monsieur D— shivered and immediately asked, 'Of what?' Angina.'

The little old man uttered an 'Ah!' of relief. He went on, 'She was too fat, too stout. That woman must have eaten too much. When I get to her age I will keep a better eye on myself.'

He was two years older than her, but he only admitted to being seventy.

A few months later it was Henri Brissot's turn. Monsieur D— was very moved. It was a man this time, a thin one, just his age, within three months or so, and careful. He didn't dare ask more, waiting for the doctor to speak, and he was feeling uneasy:

'Ah, he died, like that, all of a sudden? He was very well last week. He must have been careless in some way, don't you think, doctor?'

The doctor, who was enjoying himself, replied, 'I don't believe so. His children told me he had been very sensible.'

Then, unable to hold out, trembling with anxiety, Monsieur D— asked, 'But ... but ... what did he die of, then?'

'Pleurisy.'

There was an eruption of true joy. The little old man clapped his dry hands together: 'Lord, didn't I tell you he had done something careless? You don't get pleurisy for no reason. He might have wanted a breath of air after his dinner, and the cold got to his chest. Pleurisy! That's an accident; it's not even an illness! It's only crazy people who die of pleurisy!'

And he ate his dinner merrily, talking about the old people who remained:

'There are only fifteen of them now, but they're the strong ones, aren't they? Life is like that. The weakest go first. Those who make it past thirty have a good chance of getting to sixty; those who make it past sixty often reach eighty; and those who make it past eighty almost always achieve a hundred, because they are the strongest, the wisest, the toughest.'

Another two passed away during the year, one of dysentery and the other of breathlessness. Monsieur D— was greatly entertained by the death of the first one: 'Dysentery is the disease of the incautious! The Devil take it! You should have watched his diet, doctor.'

As for the one carried off by breathlessness, that could only be because of heart disease, undiagnosed until then.

But one evening the doctor announced the death of Paul Timonet, a sort of dried-up bag of bones whom it was dearly hoped would be good publicity as a centenarian for the spa.

When Monsieur D— asked, as was his custom, 'What did he die of?', the doctor replied, 'Upon my word, I really don't know.'

'What do you mean, you don't know? You always know. Didn't he have some organic lesion?'

The doctor shook his head, 'No, none.'

'Perhaps some problem with his liver, or his kidneys?'

'No, they were all sound.'

'Did you watch carefully to see if his stomach was functioning regularly? An attack often comes from bad digestion.'

'He didn't have an attack.'

Monsieur D— was very perplexed and getting worried. 'But look here. He must have died of something. So what was it, in your opinion?'

The doctor raised his arms. 'I have no idea, absolutely none. He is dead because he is dead, that's all.'

Then Monsieur D— asked in an emotional voice, 'What age was he exactly? I don't remember.'

'Eighty-nine.'

Astonished and relieved, the little old man cried out, 'Eighty-nine! So he didn't die of old age, after all? ...'

'Malades et médecins' was first published on 11 May 1884 in Gil Blas. This is the first English translation.

The Rondoli Sisters

I

'No,' said Pierre Jouvenet, 'I don't know Italy. I have tried to enter it twice, but I found myself stopped at the frontier in such a way that it was always impossible to get any further. And yet these two attempts have given me a charming idea of the customs of that beautiful country. I have yet to make the acquaintance of the towns, the museums, the masterpieces that crowd that land. I will try once more, at the first opportunity, to venture into that impassable territory.

'You don't understand? I will explain.'

It was in 1874 that I first felt the desire to see Venice, Florence, Rome and Naples. It happened around 15 June, when the powerful rising of the sap in spring fills the heart with the ardour to travel and to love.

Actually I am not a traveller. Moving from place to place seems to me tiring and pointless. The nights on the railway, your sleep disturbed the rattling of the carriages, the headaches and the stiffness in your limbs, waking exhausted in this rolling box, the feeling of having dirty skin, the smuts flying into your eyes and hair, the smell of coal on everything you eat, the dreadful dinners in the draughty buffet – to my mind these make a detestable start to a pleasure trip.

After this introduction in the Express train, we face the melancholy of the hotel, the big hotel full of people and so empty, the distressing, unfamiliar room, the suspect bed! I am more concerned about my bed than anything else. It is a sanctuary from life. The weary flesh is delivered up to it naked to rest and become rejuvenated in the warmth of down and the whiteness of the sheets.

There are to be found the most pleasant hours of our existence, the hours of love and sleep. The bed is sacred. We should respect, venerate and love it as one of the best and sweetest things on earth.

I cannot lift the sheet of a bed in a hotel without a shiver of disgust. What was done in it the previous night? What unclean, repulsive people have slept on these mattresses? I think of all the fearful people one jostles every day, the ugly hunchbacks, the pimply skin, the black hands that make you think of the feet, and the rest. I think of encounters with people who assail your nose with the sickening smells of garlic and humanity. I think of the misshapen, the purulent, the sweating invalids, all the ugliness and dirtiness of man.

All that has gone on in this bed where I am going to sleep. I feel sickened as I slip my feet into it.

And the hotel dinners, the long table d'hôte set dinners among all these grotesque and mind-numbing people; or the fearful solitary dinners at the little restaurant table, staring at some poor candle topped with a lampshade.

How about the agonizing evenings in the unknown city? Is there anything more miserable than night falling on a foreign town? You make your way blindly in the midst of a hustle and bustle that seems as surprising as in a dream. You look at faces you have never seen before and will never see again, you listen to voices talking about things which mean nothing to you, in a language you do not even understand. You experience the awful feeling of being lost. Your heart tightens, your legs are weak, your spirits downcast. You walk as if you are trying to escape, you walk to avoid going back to the hotel where you would find yourself still more lost because there is your place, the place you paid for but which belongs to everyone, and you end up subsiding on to a chair in a brightly lit café, whose lamps and gilded decorations crush you a thousand times more heavily than the shadows of the street. Then, faced with a foaming beer fetched by the rushing waiter, you feel so abominably alone that a sort of madness grips you, a need to leave, to go somewhere else, never mind where, rather than stay at this marble table under this bright chandelier. And you suddenly realise that you are truly, always and everywhere alone in the world, and that in familiar places familiar encounters only give you the illusion of human brotherhood. It is in these hours of abandon, of black isolation in far-off cities that one thinks broadly, clearly and deeply. It is then that you grasp the whole of life in a single glance, detached from the posture of eternal hope, the deception of acquired habits and the expectation of happiness one always dreams about.

It is in going a long way away that you really understand how everything is near and brief and empty; it is in looking for the unknown that you really realize how everything is mediocre and fleeting; it is in travelling the world that you really see how small it is and invariably more or less the same.

Oh! the gloomy evenings of walking at random through unknown streets, I know them. I am more afraid of those than of anything.

So since I did not at all want to go alone on this journey to Italy, I decided to take my friend Paul Pavilly with me.

You know Paul. As far as he is concerned the world, life, is woman. There are many men of that sort. His existence seems to him to be illuminated, poeticized by the presence of women. The world is only habitable because they are there; the sun is warm and bright because it shines on them. The air is sweet to breathe because it glides over their skin and makes the little hairs on their temples fly about. The moon is charming because it makes them dream and lends a languid charm to love. Certainly all Paul's acts are motivated by women; all his thoughts are directed towards them, as are all his efforts and all his hopes.

A poet has been withering about that kind of man:

> Je déteste surtout le barde à l'oeil humide
> Qui regarde une étoile en murmurant un nom
> Et pour qui la nature immense serait vide
> S'il ne portait en croupe ou Lisette ou Ninon.
>
> Ces gens-là sont charmants qui se donnent la peine,
> Afin qu'on s'intéresse à ce pauvre univers,
> D'attacher des jupons aux arbres de la plaine
> Et la cornette blanche au front des coteaux verts.
>
> Certe ils n'ont pas compris tes musiques divines,
> Eternelle nature aux frémissantes voix,
> Ceux qui ne vont pas seuls par les creuses ravines
> Et rêvent d'une femme au bruit que font les bois!*

---

* Louis Bouilhet, Flaubert's friend, and very often quoted by Maupassant.
'Above all I hate the bard with humid eye/Who gazes at a star while murmuring a name, /For whom vast nature would be void/If it brought no Lisette or Ninon on its rump.
'Those people are charming who go to the trouble,/ So one can find interest in this poor universe, /Of attaching petticoats to the trees in the fields/ And a white mob-cap on the forehead of the green hillsides.
'Certainly they have not understood your divine music,/ Eternal nature with vibrating voices,/ Those who do not go alone through the deep valleys/ And dream of a woman to the sounds of the woods.'

When I spoke to Paul about Italy, he absolutely refused at first to leave Paris, but I got to telling him of the adventure of travel; I told him how the Italian women were said to be delightful; I made him hope for refined pleasures at Naples, thanks to an introduction I had to a certain Signore Michel Amoroso, whose contacts were very useful for travellers; and he let himself be tempted.

II

We took the Express on a Thursday evening, 26 June. Few people go to the Midi at that time of year; we were alone in the carriage, both of us ill-humoured, annoyed at leaving Paris, lamenting that we had given in to the idea of travelling, already missing the freshness of Marly, the beauty of the Seine, the tranquillity of the river banks, the lovely days idling in a boat, the lovely evenings dozing at the waterside, waiting for night to fall.

Paul settled himself in his corner and, once the train had started, declared, 'It's a stupid idea to be going there.'

As it was too late for him to change his mind, I replied, 'You shouldn't have come.'

There was no reply. But I wanted to laugh as I looked at him, he looked so furious. He certainly looks like a squirrel. Actually, underneath the human lines all of us retain in our features an animal type, like the mark of our primitive race. How many people have the muzzle of a bulldog, the head of a goat, rabbit, fox, horse, cow! Paul is a squirrel become man. He has the animal's bright eyes, its red hair, its pointed nose, its small, fine, supple and restless body, and then there is a mysterious resemblance in his general demeanour. I'm not sure what it is – a similarity of gesture, movement, manner of which he perhaps retains some memory.

Eventually we both slept the noisy sleep that you get on railways, broken by cramps in the arms and neck and the sudden halts of the train.

We happened to wake up as we were going alongside the Rhone. And soon the continuous sound of cicadas coming through the windows, a cry like the voice of the hot earth, the song of Provence, flung in our faces, our lungs, our souls the gaiety of the Midi, the taste of burnt soil, the stony and bright home of the gnarled olive tree with its verdigris foliage.

As the train drew to a halt again, a porter began to run along the train calling out a sonorous 'Valence', a true 'Valence', with that accent, the full-blown accent that once again brought us the taste of Provence which the grating of the cicadas had already invoked.

Until we reached Marseille there was nothing new.

We got out and went to the buffet for lunch.

When we got back into our carriage we found a woman settled in it.

Paul threw me a delighted look and with an automatic gesture curled his short moustache, then ran his fingers lightly through his hair, which was very dishevelled from the night of travelling. Then he sat down opposite the unknown woman.

Every time I find myself, either when I am going somewhere or socially, confronted with a new face I become obsessed with making guesses about the mind, the intelligence, the character that is hiding behind those features.

This was a young woman, quite young and pretty, certainly a girl from the Midi. She had superb eyes, admirable black hair, wavy, a little frizzy, so bushy, vigorous and long that it seemed heavy, so that just looking at it gave the impression of weight on her head. Dressed with both elegance and a certain southern bad taste, she seemed slightly vulgar. The regular features of her face did not have the grace, the finish found in people of elegant race, the light delicacy that the sons of aristocrats acquire at birth like the inherited mark of finer blood.

She was wearing bracelets that were too big to be gold, earrings adorned with clear stones too big to be diamonds; her whole person conveyed a certain commonness. You could guess that she would speak too loudly, shouting all the time with exuberant gestures.

The train pulled out.

She remained motionless in her seat, her eyes fixed before her with the scowling pose of an angry woman. She had not even glanced at us.

Paul began to chat to me, saying things for effect, putting on a show of conversation to attract interest the way shopkeepers display their choicest goods to arouse desire.

But she seemed not to hear.

'Toulon! Ten minute stop! Buffet!' shouted the porter.

Paul signalled to me to get out and, once on the platform, said, 'Tell me, who can she be?'

I began to laugh. 'I don't know. It's all the same to me.'

He was very keen. 'She's damned pretty and fresh, that hussy. What eyes! But she doesn't look pleased. She must have problems; she's not paying attention to anything.'

I murmured, 'You are wasting your time.'

But he was annoyed. 'I'm not trying, old man; I find this woman very pretty, that's all. Could we speak to her? But what can we say? Go on, you, don't you have any idea? Can't you imagine who she might be?'

'Good gracious, no. However, I would guess she's an actress rejoining her company after an amorous escapade.'

He looked offended, as though I had said something to upset

him, and continued, 'What makes you think that? On the contrary, I think she looks very respectable.'

I replied, 'Look at her bracelets, old man, and the earrings, and her outfit. I wouldn't be surprised if she were a dancer, or perhaps even a circus rider, but more likely a dancer. Her whole person somehow smells of the theatre.'

This idea decidedly did not suit him. 'She is too young, old man, she is barely twenty.'

'But, my dear chap, there are a good many things you can do before you're twenty, dancing and declaiming speeches among them, not to mention yet others which may be her sole occupation.'

'Travellers for the Nice and Vintimille Express, rejoin your carriages!' shouted the porter.

We had to get back in. Our companion was eating an orange. She decidedly did not look refined. She had opened her handkerchief on her knees; her way of tearing off the golden peel, opening her mouth to put whole quarters between her lips, spitting the pips out of the window, betrayed the habits and gestures of an entirely common education.

Moreover she seemed grumpier than ever, and she quickly swallowed her fruit with a furious air which was quite comical.

Paul was devouring her with a look, searching for something to do to attract her attention, to arouse her curiosity. He began to chat with me, coming up with a succession of refined ideas, familiarly quoting well-known names. She took no notice at all of his efforts.

We passed Fréjus, Saint-Raphael. The train was running through a veritable garden, a paradise of roses, through groves of orange and lemon trees in full bloom, bearing white blossoms and golden fruit at the same time, through the kingdom of perfumes and homeland of flowers that is the lovely coastline between Marseille and Genoa.

June is the right time to follow this coast, where all the most beautiful flowers grow, free, wild, in narrow valleys and on the hillsides. Everywhere you keep seeing roses, fields, plains, hedges, groves of roses. They climb up the walls, open up on the roofs, scale trees, burst open among the leaves, white, red, yellow, tiny or enormous, slight and single in a costume of one colour, or fully double, giving a heavy and brilliant display.

Their strong scent, their pervasive scent thickens the air, making it delectable and languorous. And the still more penetrating smell of open orange blossom seems to sweeten the air one breathes, making of it a delicacy for the sense of smell.

The great coast with its brown rocks stretches out ahead of us, washed by the motionless Mediterranean. The sultry summer sun spreads a sheet of fire over the mountains, on the long sandy water's edge, on the hard and fixed blue of the sea. The train carries on, going into tunnels beneath the headlands, slipping over the undulations of the hills, skirting the water on cornices with wall-like drops; there is a gentle, vaguely salty smell, a smell of drying seaweed sometimes mingled with the heavy, disturbing odour of the flowers.

But Paul was seeing nothing, looking at nothing, feeling nothing. The woman traveller had all his attention.

At Cannes, wanting to talk to me once more, he signalled to get out again.

Hardly out of the carriage, he took my arm. 'She is ravishing, you know. Look at her eyes. And her hair, old man, I've never seen hair like it!'

I said to him, 'Come on, calm down; or else go in for the attack if that's your intention. She doesn't look impregnable, even though she seems a bit peevish.'

He went on, 'Could you manage to talk to her? I can't find anything to say. I'm foolishly timid, for a start. I've never known how to approach a woman in the street. I follow them, I go round and round, I approach them, and I never find the words I need. Once only did I make an attempt at conversation. As it was very obvious that my approach was expected, and as it was absolutely essential that I say something, I stammered, "Are you well, madam?" She laughed in my face and I fled.'

I promised Paul to use all my skill to start up a conversation, and when we had resumed our places I politely asked our neighbour, 'Does tobacco smoke bother you, madam?'

She replied, '*Non capisco.*'

She was Italian! I felt a desperate urge to laugh. Since Paul did not know a word of the language, I would have to act as his interpreter. I was ready to assume my role. So I enunciated in Italian, 'I was asking you, madam, if tobacco smoke bothered you in the slightest degree?'

She gave me a furious look. '*Che mi fa!*'

She had neither turned her head nor raised her eyes to me, and I was very puzzled, not knowing whether I should take this 'What do I care!' as permission, a refusal, sheer indifference or a simple 'Leave me alone.'

I went on, 'Madam, if the smell bothers you in the slightest degree …?'

Then she replied, '*Mica,*' with an intonation which meant 'Don't bother me!' All the same it was permission, and I said to Paul, 'You may smoke.' He was looking at me with those amazed eyes you have when you are trying to understand people standing before you speaking a foreign language. He asked with an utterly comical expression, 'What did you say to her?'

'I asked her if we could smoke.'

'So she doesn't know any French?'

'Not a word.'

'What did she reply?'

'That she permitted us to do whatever we pleased.'

And I lit my cigar.

Paul went on, 'Is that all she said?'

'My dear fellow, if you had counted her words you would have noted that she said just six of them, of which two were to let me know she didn't understand French. That leaves four. However, with four words you cannot really say a great deal.'

Paul seemed thoroughly unhappy, disappointed, confused.

But suddenly the Italian girl asked me in that same discontented tone that seemed natural to her, 'Do you know what time we arrive in Genoa?'

I replied, 'At eleven o'clock at night, madam.' Then, after a minute's silence, I added, 'We are also going to Genoa, my friend and I, and if we could do anything for you during the journey, I assure you we would be most happy.'

As she did not answer, I insisted, 'You are alone, and should you need our services ...' She uttered another '*mica*' so harshly that I abruptly fell silent.

Paul asked, 'What did she say?'

'She said she found you charming.'

But he wasn't in the mood for jokes, and he asked me curtly not to make fun of him. So I translated both the young woman's question and my gallant proposition that had been so roundly rejected.

He was quite as agitated as a squirrel in a cage. He said, 'If we could find out which hotel she is going to, we could go to the same one. So try to ask her some astute questions and create a new reason to talk to her.'

It really wasn't easy and I did not know what to come up with, though I wanted to get to know this difficult person myself.

We passed Nice, Monaco, Menton, and the train stopped at the frontier for the luggage to be checked.

Even though I have a horror of ill-bred people who eat their lunch and dinner in the carriage, I went and bought a whole load of provisions in a final effort to arouse our companion's greed. It was obvious that in ordinary circumstances this girl must be easily approachable. Some annoyance or other was making her irritable, but perhaps it would only take a trivial thing, an awakened desire, a word, a well-phrased offer to stop her frowning, to persuade her, to conquer her.

We were moving off again. The three of us were still alone. I spread out my supplies on the seat, cut up the chicken, elegantly arranged the slices of ham on a paper, then carefully laid out our dessert right next to the young woman: strawberries, plums, cherries, cakes and sweetmeats.

When she saw we were beginning to eat she pulled a piece of chocolate and two croissants out of a little bag and began to crunch the crusty bread and the chocolate bar with her beautiful sharp teeth.

Paul said to me in a low voice, 'Offer her something, then!'

'I intend to, my dear fellow, but it's not easy to begin.'

However, she was casting the occasional sidelong look at our provisions, and I really felt she would be hungry again once she had finished her two croissants. So I let her finish her frugal dinner. Then I asked her:

'Would you be so gracious, madam, as to accept some of this fruit?'

Once more she replied, '*Mica!*', but in a less unpleasant voice than during the day, and I pressed her, 'Then would you allow me to offer you a little wine? I see you have had nothing to drink. It is wine from your native land, Italian wine, and since we are now in your country we would be very pleased to see a pretty Italian mouth accept an offer from her neighbours, the French.'

She shook her head, gently, meaning to refuse and wanting to accept, and once more she enunciated *mica*, but now an almost polite *mica*. I took the little bottle wrapped in straw in the Italian style; I filled a glass and presented it to her.

'Drink it,' I said to her. 'It will be our welcome to your country.'

She took the glass with a discontented look and emptied it in one go, as though she were tortured by thirst, then she gave it back to me without saying thank you.

Then I offered her the cherries: 'Take them, madam, please. You know it would give us great pleasure.'

From her corner she was looking at all the fruit spread out beside her, and she announced so quickly that I had great difficulty in hearing it, 'A *me non piacciono ne le ciliegie ne le susine; amo soltanto le fragole.*'

'What is she saying?' Paul asked at once.

'She says that she doesn't like either cherries or plums, but only the strawberries.'

I took the newspaper packet filled with wild strawberries and put it on her lap. She immediately began to eat them very quickly, grabbing them up with the tips of her fingers and throwing them, from a little too far, into her mouth as it opened to receive them in an attractive and charming way.

When she had finished the little red pile, which we had watched dwindle, melt and disappear in a few minutes with the quick movement of her hands, I asked her, 'What may I offer you now?'

She replied, 'I would like a little chicken.'

And she devoured at least half of the chicken, which she dismembered with great motions of her jaw like a true carnivore.

Then she decided to take the cherries, which she didn't like, then the plums, then the cakes, and then she said, 'I've had enough,' and huddled into her corner.

I was becoming very amused, and I wanted to get her to eat more, so I multiplied my compliments and my offers in an attempt to persuade her. But she suddenly became furious again, and threw in my face a repeated '*Mica*' so dreadful that I didn't dare to disturb her digestion any more.

I turned towards my friend. 'My poor Paul, I think that is all we'll get for our efforts.'

Night was coming on, a hot summer night that was falling slowly, spreading its warm shadows over the weary, smouldering land. Here and there in the distance, towards the sea, lanterns were lighting up on the headlands and the tops of the promontories; the stars too were beginning to appear on the darkening horizon, and at times I confused them with the lighthouses.

The scent of the orange trees was becoming more penetrating; you breathed it in ecstatically, expanding your lungs to drink it in deeply. Something sweet, delicious, divine seemed to be floating in the balmy air.

All at once I noticed along the railway line under the trees, in the shadows which were now quite black, something like a shower of stars. You might have said they were leaping drops of light, flying, playing and running through the leaves, little stars fallen from the sky to have a party on earth. They were fireflies, glowing and dancing a strange fiery ballet in the perfumed air.

One of them happened to come into our carriage and began to dart about casting its intermittent light, no sooner extinguished than lit again. I covered our lamp with its blue shade and I was watching the fantastic fly coming and going with the caprice of its glowing flight. All at once it landed in the black hair of our neighbour, who was dozing after her dinner. Paul was in silent ecstasy, his eyes fixed on the brilliant spot that was twinkling like a living jewel on the brow of the sleeping woman.

She woke up at about a quarter to eleven, still wearing the little illuminated creature in her hair. I said, when I saw her stirring, 'We are almost at Genoa, madam.' She murmured, without answering me, as though obsessed with a fixed and embarrassing idea, 'What am I going to do now?'

Then, suddenly, she asked me, 'Do you want me to come with you?'

I was struck with such stupefaction that I did not understand.

'What, with us? What do you mean?'

She repeated, in a more and more furious tone, 'Do you want me to go with you straight away?'

'That suits me; but where would you like to go? Where do you want me to take you?'

She shrugged her shoulders with supreme indifference.

'Wherever you like! It's all the same to me.'

Twice she repeated: '*Che mi fa?*'

'Well … if we're going to a hotel?'

She said most contemptuously, 'Well then, let's go to a hotel.'

My friend's look of panic-stricken surprise helped me recover my composure. He stammered, 'With us? But where? Why? How?'

'How should I know? She has just made this strange proposal in the most irritated voice. I replied that we were going to the hotel; she answered, "Well then, let's go to the hotel." She can't have a sou. All the same, she has a peculiar way of getting to know people.'

Paul, agitated and quivering, cried, 'But of course, yes, I would like that, tell her we will take her wherever she pleases.' Then he hesitated a second, and went on in a troubled voice, 'But we would need to know who she is with. Is she with you or me?'

I turned towards the Italian girl, who had relapsed into complete indifference and did not even seem to be listening to us, and said to her, 'We would be very happy, madam, to take you with us. Only, my friend would like to know if you would like to take my arm or his?'

She gazed at me with her big dark eyes and answered with vague surprise, '*Che mi fa?*'

I explained: 'I believe that in Italy the friend who takes care of all of a woman's desires, looks after all her wishes and satisfies all her fancies is called a *patito*. Which of us two do you want as your *patito*?'

Without hesitation she answered, 'You!'

I turned to Paul. 'She has chosen me, my dear chap, you are out of luck.'

He declared in an infuriated voice, 'So much the better for you.'

Then, when he had thought about it for a few minutes, he said, 'Are you determined to bring that slut with you? She will ruin our trip. What are we going to do with this woman who looks like I don't know what? They won't even let us into a decent hotel!'

But I was just beginning to get a better opinion of the Italian girl than I had at first; and now I was determined, yes, determined to take her with me. I was even delighted at the thought, and I could already feel those little thrills of anticipation that the prospect of an amorous night sends running through the veins.

I answered, 'We have accepted, my dear fellow. It is too late to turn back. It was you who first advised me to answer "Yes".'

He grumbled, 'It's stupid! Anyway, do as you like.'

The train was whistling, slowing down; we had arrived.

I got out of the carriage, then held my hand out to my new girlfriend. She jumped lightly to the ground and I offered her my arm, which she seemed to take with repugnance. Once the luggage had been identified and claimed, we set out across the town. Paul was walking in silence, with nervous steps.

I said to him, 'Which hotel shall we go to? It might be tricky to go to the City of Paris with a woman, especially with our Italian friend.'

Paul interrupted, 'Yes, with an Italian girl who looks more like a tart than a duchess. Anyway, it's none of my business. Do as you like!'

I still could not decide. I had written to the City of Paris to reserve our suite ... but now ... I didn't know what to do.

Two porters were following us with our trunks. I said, 'You had better go on ahead. Tell them we are on our way. And give the manager to understand that I am with a ... woman friend, and that we would like a quite separate suite for the three of us, so we don't have to become involved with the other guests. He will understand, and we will make our decision in the light of his reply.'

Paul grumbled, 'Thank you, but the assignment and the role don't suit me. I didn't come here to sort out your rooms and your pleasures.'

But I insisted, 'Look here, my dear chap, don't get annoyed. It's most certainly better to stay at a good hotel than a bad one, and it really isn't difficult to go and ask the manager for three separate bedrooms, with a dining room.'

I emphasised the three, and that convinced him.

So he went on ahead and I saw him go in through the big door-way of a fine hotel while I stayed on the other side of the street, trailing my mute Italian girl, and followed step by step by the porters with our luggage.

156

Paul eventually came back wearing a face as sullen as my Italian girlfriend's. 'It's done,' he said, 'they'll have us; but there are only two bedrooms. You will have to deal with that as best you can.'

I followed him, feeling ashamed at entering the hotel in such dubious company.

We did indeed have two rooms, separated by a little sitting room. I asked for a cold supper to be sent up, then I turned in some confusion to the Italian girl.

'We could only get two rooms, madam. Choose which one you would like.'

She replied with the eternal '*Che mi fa?*' So I picked up her little black wooden box, a real servant's trunk, and carried it to the room on the right which I chose for her … for us. A square of paper had been glued to her trunk, and on it was written in a French hand: 'Mademoiselle Francesca Rondoli, Genoa.'

I asked, 'Are you called Francesca?'

She nodded without answering.

I went on, 'We are going to have supper soon. In the meantime, perhaps you would like to tidy yourself up?'

She replied with a '*mica*', a word as frequently on her lips as the '*che mi fa*'. I insisted, 'After a railway journey it is so pleasant to get clean.'

Then it occurred to me that perhaps she did not have the indispensable feminine things, for she certainly seemed to be in an unusual position, as though she were getting out of some unpleasant adventure, and I brought out my toilet case.

I reached for all the little instruments of cleanliness it had in it: a nail brush, a new toothbrush – I always take a selection of them with me – my scissors, my nail files, sponges. I opened a bottle of eau-de-Cologne, a bottle of ambered lavender water and a little bottle of Newmownhay* to give her a choice. I opened my pot of powder with its light swansdown puff. I laid one of my good towels across the water jug and put a new piece of soap next to the bowl.

She followed my movements with her big angry eyes, giving no sign that she was surprised or pleased at my attentions.

I said to her, 'There is everything you need. I will let you know when supper is ready.'

And I went back into the sitting room. Paul had taken possession of the other bedroom and shut himself in it, so I was left alone to wait.

A waiter was coming and going, bringing plates and glasses. He slowly laid the table, then put a cold chicken on it and announced that I was served.

I knocked gently on Miss Rondoli's door. She cried, 'Come in.' I went in. A suffocating smell of perfume assaulted me, that strong, thick smell of hairdresser's salons.

The Italian girl was sitting on her trunk in the pose of an unhappy thinker, or a dismissed maid. I could see at a glance what she understood by tidying herself up. The towel remained folded on the still full water jug. The dry soap was intact, still next to the empty bowl; but you might have thought the young woman had drunk half the bottles of toilet water. The eau-de-Cologne had been spared, since only about a third of the bottle was missing; but, to compensate, she had consumed an astonishing quantity of ambered lavender water and Newmownhay. A cloud of powder, a vague white mist, seemed to be floating in the air, so liberally had she daubed her face and neck with it. She had a sort of frost of it in her eyelashes, in her eyebrows and on her temples, her cheeks were plastered with it and you could see it in deep layers in all the

---

* In English in the original; a fashionable perfume of the time.

creases of her face, on the sides of her nose, in the dimple on her chin, in the corners of her eyes.

When she got up she distributed such a violent smell that I felt I was getting a migraine.

We sat down at the table for our supper. Paul had worked himself up into an abominable mood. I could only get out of him words of blame, irritable opinions or unpleasant compliments.

Miss Francesca ate like a horse. As soon as she had finished her meal she dozed on the sofa. I contemplated with some anxiety the arrival of the decisive moment for sharing out the rooms. I resolved to bring matters to a head and, sitting beside the Italian girl, chivalrously kissed her hand.

She half opened her weary eyes and gave me a sleepy and still discontented glance from under her raised eyelids.

I said to her, 'Since we only have two bedrooms, will you let me come with you in yours?'

She replied, 'Do as you like. It's all the same to me. *Che mi fa?*'

This indifference hurt me. 'So you won't mind if I come with you?'

'It's all the same to me, do as you like.'

'Would you like to go to bed straight away?'

'Yes, I would like that; I'm tired.'

She got up, yawned, held out her hand to Paul, who took it angrily, and I led the way into our room.

Anxiety was haunting me. 'Here,' I said to her again, 'is everything you need.'

And I carefully poured half the water jug into the bowl myself, and put the towel next to the soap.

Then I went back to Paul. As soon as I came in he declared, 'You've brought along a fine bitch!'

I replied, laughing, 'That's sour grapes, my dear chap.'

He went on, with sly malice, 'You'll see if you catch a dose, old man.'

I shuddered, gripped by the tormenting fear that pursues us after suspect love affairs, the fear that spoils the charming encounters, unexpected caresses and kisses gathered at random. Still, I put on a brave face. 'Go on, that girl isn't a harlot.'

But he'd got me, the wretch! He had seen the shadow of anxiety pass across my face: 'Do you really think you know her? You're amazing! You pick up an Italian woman in a railway carriage, travelling alone, and with really extraordinary cynicism she offers to sleep with you in the first hotel you come to. You take her there. And you claim she is not a tart! You're trying to fool yourself that you are running no more danger this evening than if you were sharing a bed with a ... woman with chicken pox.'

And he laughed with his unpleasant, offended laugh. I sat down, tortured by anxiety. What was I going to do? He was right. A terrible battle was raging within me between fear and desire.

He went on, 'Do as you like, I've warned you; don't complain about the results.'

I saw such ironic gaiety, such pleasure in vengeance in his eyes, he was so heartily making fun of me that I hesitated no longer. I held out my hand to him. 'Goodnight,' I said. 'À *vaincre sans péril, on triomphe sans gloire.** And my word, my dear fellow, the victory is worth the danger.'

With that I marched into Francesca's bedroom with a firm step.

I stopped in the doorway, surprised, filled with wonder. She was already sleeping, quite naked, on the bed. Sleep had surprised her as she had just got undressed, and she was lying in the charming pose of Titian's wonderful woman.

---

* Corneille, *Le Cid*, II.2: 'Victory without peril is triumph without glory.'

160

She seemed to have lain down wearily, to take off her stockings, for they were still on the sheet; then she had thought of something, no doubt something pleasant, for she had lingered a little before bringing her daydream to an end and getting up, then, gently closing her eyes, she had lost consciousness. A nightdress was lying on a chair, embroidered at the collar, bought ready-made in a clothes shop, a debutante's luxury.

She was charming, young, firm and fresh.

What is prettier than a sleeping woman? That body, whose every con tour is gentle, whose every curve is seductive, whose every soft protuberance troubles the heart, seems designed to lie immobile on a bed. That sinuous line which curves into the side, rises at the hip, then descends the light and graceful slope of the leg to finish so prettily at the end of the foot, can only really be portrayed in all its exquisite charm when stretched out on the sheets of a couch.

In an instant I would have forgotten my friend's prudent advice; but suddenly, turning towards the wash-stand, I saw everything in the same state I had left it in; and I sat down, most uneasy, tortured by indecision.

I certainly stayed there a long time, a very long time, an hour perhaps, without coming to a decision either to be brave or to take flight. In any case retreat was impossible, and I either had to spend the night on a chair, or also take to the bed, quite at my own risk.

As for sleeping, either here or there, I couldn't think of it, as my head was too agitated and my eyes too busy.

I was constantly moving, feverish, throbbing, uncomfortable, excessively on edge. Then I succumbed to the reasoning of a man on the point of surrender: 'Going to bed commits me to nothing. One always gets a better rest on a mattress than a chair.'

I slowly undressed; then, climbing over the sleeping girl, I stretched out against the wall, turning my back to temptation.

And again I stayed there a long time, a very long time, without sleep.

Suddenly my neighbour woke up. She opened astonished and still discontented eyes then, noticing that she was naked, she got up and quietly put on her nightdress, with as little concern as though I had not been there.

Then ... my word ... I took advantage of the situation, which didn't seem to bother her in the slightest bit. And she went placidly back to sleep, her head resting on her right arm.

I began to meditate on human weakness and imprudence. Then at last I dozed off.

She got dressed early, like a woman used to having jobs to do in the morning. The movement she made as she got up woke me; and I watched her between half-closed eyelids.

She was coming and going, in no hurry, as though surprised at having nothing to do. Then she returned to the washstand, and in a minute she had emptied all that remained of the perfume in the bottles. She also used some water, it is true, but not much.

Then when she was completely dressed she sat down again on her trunk and, one knee in her hands, she went back to thinking.

At that point I pretended to notice her and said, 'Good morning, Francesca.'

She muttered, no more graciously than the day before, 'Good morning.'

I asked, 'Did you sleep well?'

She nodded without replying, and jumping to the ground I went to kiss her.

She held out her face with the irritated gesture of a child being caressed against its will. So I took her tenderly in my arms (the wine having been drawn, I would have been really stupid to drink no more of it) and slowly planted my lips on the big angry eyes she was closing from boredom beneath my kisses, on her clear cheeks, on the fleshy lips which she was turning away.

I said to her, 'Don't you like it, then, when you are kissed?'

She answered, '*Mica*.'

I sat down on the trunk beside her and passed my arm under hers. '*Mica! mica! mica!* for everything. From now on I shall call you nothing but Miss Mica.'

For the first time I thought I saw the shadow of a smile on her mouth, but it passed so quickly I could easily have been mistaken.

'But if you always answer *mica* I won't know what to try to please you. Look, what shall we do today?'

She hesitated as though the ghost of a desire might have passed through her head, then she announced listlessly, 'I don't mind, whatever you like.'

'Well, Miss Mica, we will take a carriage and go for a drive.'

She murmured, 'As you like.'

Paul was waiting for us in the dining room with the bored expression worn by the third party in a love affair. I put on a show of delight and shook his hand with a vigour that bespoke triumph.

He asked, 'What are you thinking of doing?'

I replied, 'Well, first we will go round the town a little, then we could take a carriage to see some of the surroundings.'

Lunch was a silent affair, then we went off through the streets to visit the museums. I pulled Francesca along on my arm from palace to palace. We went through the Spinola Palace, the Doria Palace, the Marcello Durazzo Palace, the Red Palace and the White Palace. She looked at nothing, except sometimes she would lift weary, listless eyes to the works of art. Paul, fuming, was following us muttering unpleasant things. Then a carriage took us round the countryside, all three of us sitting in silence.

Then we returned for dinner.

The next day it was the same, and again the next day.

On the third day Paul said to me, 'I am going to leave you, you know; I'm not going to stay for three weeks watching you make love to that slut!'

This left me very confused and very embarrassed for, to my great surprise, I had become attached to Francesca in a peculiar sort of way. Man is stupid and weak, carried away by a whim, and spineless whenever his senses are aroused or subjugated. I was attached to a girl whom I didn't know, who was always discontented and taciturn. I liked her grumpy face, her pouting mouth, her bored expression; I liked her tired gestures, her contemptuous consents, even the indifference of her caresses. A secret tie, the secret tie of bestial love, the secret attachment of unsated possession, kept me close to her. I said so to Paul, quite frankly. He treated me as if I was a fool, then said, 'Oh well, bring her along.'

However, she obstinately refused to leave Genoa, though she would not explain why. I pleaded, argued, promised; nothing would do.

And I stayed.

Paul declared he was going off alone. He even packed his trunk, but he stayed too.

Two more weeks passed.

Francesca, still silent and irritable, was living alongside me rather than with me, responding to all my desires, requests and propositions with her eternal *che mi fa* or the equally eternal *mica*.

My friend was no less angry. To all his outbursts I would reply, 'You can leave if you are bored. I am not keeping you.'

Then he would insult me, pour reproaches on me, and cry,

'Where do you suppose I could go now? We did have three weeks, and now a fortnight has gone! I can't continue the journey at this point! And as if I would go to Venice, Florence and Rome on my own! But you will pay me back for this, and more than you think. You don't bring a man from Paris to shut him in a hotel in Genoa with an Italian harlot!'

I said to him calmly, 'Well, go back to Paris then.' And he shouted, 'That's what I'm going to do, and I'll be gone by tomorrow.'

But the next day he stayed, like the day before, still furious and swearing.

They had got to know us now in the streets where we wandered from morning to night, through the narrow streets without pavements in a town that resembles a huge stone labyrinth pierced with tunnel-like corridors. We would pass along passages through which raging currents of air blew, and down traverses squeezed between walls so high you could hardly see the sky. Sometimes French people would turn round, astonished to recognize fellow countrymen in the company of this cross girl in garish clothes, whose demeanour really did seem peculiar, out of place, compromising even, walking between the two of us.

She would lean on my arm, looking at nothing. Why did she stay with me, with us, when we seemed to give her so little pleasure? Who was she? Where did she come from? What did she do? Did she have a plan, an idea? Or did she live aimlessly, guided by encounters and chance? I sought in vain to understand her, to penetrate her, to explain her. The more I got to know her the more she surprised me, like an enigma. She was certainly no trollop, making a profession of love. She seemed to me more like the daughter of a poor family, seduced, abducted, then abandoned, and now lost. But what did she think would become of her? What was she expecting? She didn't at all seem to me to be trying to make a conquest of me, or to make any actual profit out of me.

I tried to question her, to talk to her about her childhood and her family. She did not answer. I would stay with her, my heart free and my flesh tormented, not at all tired of holding her in my arms, this scornful and superb female, coupling like an animal, gripped or rather seduced by the senses, overcome by a kind of sensual charm, the young, healthy, powerful charm that emanated from her, from her delectable skin and the robust lines of her body.

Another week went by. The end of my trip was coming closer as I had to be back in Paris on 11 July. Paul now pretty well accepted the adventure, even as he continually insulted me. As for me, I was busy thinking up pleasures, distractions, outings to amuse my mistress and my friend; I was going to endless trouble.

One day I suggested an excursion to Santa Margarita. That charming little town is set among gardens, hidden at the foot of a hill which extends far into the sea right to the village of Portofino. The three of us followed the marvellous road which runs the length of the mountain. Suddenly Francesca said to me, 'Tomorrow I will not be able to go out with you. I will go and see my relatives.'

Then she was silent. I did not question her, sure that she would not answer me.

Indeed the next day she got up very early. Then, as I did not get up, she sat at the foot of the bed and said in an embarrassed, upset, hesitant voice, 'If I have not returned by this evening, will you come and look for me?'

I answered, 'Yes, of course. Where do I have to go?'

She explained to me, 'You go along Victor Emmanuel Street, then you take Falcone Passage and the Saint Raphael Alley, you go through the furniture shop, into the courtyard, right to the end, into the building on the right, and you ask for Madame Rondoli. It's there.'

And she went. I was distinctly surprised.

On seeing me alone Paul, astounded, said hesitantly, 'Where is Francesca then?' And I told him what had just happened.

He burst out, 'Well, my dear chap, let's take advantage of the situation and leave. Our time is up in any case. Two days more or less makes no difference. *En route, en route*, pack your trunk. Let's be off!'

I refused: 'No, my dear fellow, I really can't drop the girl like that, after spending nearly three weeks with her. I have to say goodbye to her, to get her to accept some sort of gift. No, that would be behaving like a swine.'

But he didn't want to know, he pressurised me, he harassed me. Nevertheless I didn't give in.

I didn't go out all day, waiting for Francesca to return. She did not come back.

In the evening, at dinner, Paul was triumphant. 'She's the one who has dropped you, my dear chap. That's funny, that's really funny.'

I was surprised, I admit, and a little annoyed. He laughed in my face, made fun of me. 'Actually it's not a bad method, if rather primitive: "Wait for me, I'll be back." Are you going to wait a long time for her? Who knows? You might even have been naive enough to go and look for her at the address she gave you: "Madame Rondoli, if you please?" "This is not the house, Sir." I'll bet you want to go there, don't you?'

I protested, 'Not at all, my dear fellow, and I assure you that if she has not come back by tomorrow morning I am leaving on the eight o'clock express. I will have waited twenty-four hours. That's enough; my conscience will be clear.'

I spent the whole evening in a state of anxiety, a little sad, a little nervous. I really felt something for her. At midnight I went to bed. I hardly slept.

I was up at six. I woke Paul, packed my trunk, and two hours later we took the train for France.

III

Now it came about that the following year, at just the same time, I was seized by a new desire to see Italy, as one is by a recurring fever. Straight away I decided to go, for visiting Florence, Venice and Rome is surely part of a well-bred gentleman's education. Besides it provides a multitude of subjects for social conversation and gives one the ability to turn out artistic platitudes that always seem profound.

I went alone this time, and I arrived in Genoa at the same time as the previous year, but without any adventures on the way. I would stay at the same hotel, and as it happened I had the same room!

But scarcely had I got into that bed than I began to recall the memory of Francesca, who had actually been vaguely floating in my thoughts since the previous evening, haunting me with a strange persistence.

Do you know that obsession with a woman long afterwards, when you return to the place where you have loved and possessed her?

It is one of the strongest and most distressing sensations I know. It seems as if you are about to see her walk in, smile, open her arms. Her image, fleeting yet precise, stands before you, passes by, returns, disappears. She tortures you like a nightmare, takes hold of you, fills your heart, disturbs your senses with her unreal presence. The eye catches glimpses of her; the smell of her perfume pursues you; you can taste her kisses on your lips and the caress of her flesh on your skin. Yet you are alone, and you know it, and you suffer from the strange disturbance of this conjured-up phantom. And a heavy, distressing sadness envelops you. It seems as though you have just been abandoned for ever. Every object takes on an desolate meaning, casting over mind and heart a horrible impression of loneliness and abandonment. Oh, never again to set eyes upon the town, the house, the bedroom, the woods, the garden, the bench where you held in your arms a woman you loved!

In a word, I was pursued by the memory of Francesca all night and, little by little, the desire to see her again penetrated me, a confused desire at first, then more alive, more acute, burning. I decided to stay in Genoa all the following day, to try to find her again. If I didn't succeed I would take the evening train.

So, come morning I set out in search of her. I remembered perfectly well the instructions she had given me as she left me: 'Victor Emmanuel Street – Falcone Passage – Saint Raphael Alley – furniture shop – the end of the courtyard, building on the right.'

I found it all without any trouble, and I knocked on the door of a dilapidated little house. The door was opened by a fat woman, who must once have been very beautiful but was now just very dirty. Too fat, but all the same she had preserved a remarkable majesty of line. Her uncombed hair fell in locks over her forehead and shoulders, and you could see all her great ballooning body floating in a vast, stain-spattered dressing gown. She had an enormous gilt necklace round her neck and, on both wrists, superb bracelets of Genoese filigree.

She asked in a hostile tone, 'What do you want?'

I replied, 'Isn't this where Miss Francesca Rondoli lives?'

'What do you want her for?'

'I had the pleasure of meeting her last year, and I would have liked to see her again.'

The old woman looked me over with her suspicious eyes. 'Tell me where you met her.'

'Right here, in Genoa!'

'What is your name?'

I hesitated a moment, then I gave her my name. I had hardly pronounced it when the Italian woman raised her arms as though she was about to kiss me. 'Ah! you are the Frenchman. How happy I am to see you! How happy I am! But how you made the poor child suffer. She waited a month for you, sir, yes, a month. The first day she was sure you were going to come and look for her. She wanted to see if you loved her! If you knew how she cried when she realized you would not come. Yes, sir, she cried her heart out. And then she went to the hotel. You had gone. So she decided you must have continued on your journey through Italy and that you would pass through Genoa again and would look for her when you returned because she hadn't wanted to go with you. And she waited, yes, more than a month; and she was very sad, you know, very sad. I am her mother!'

I really felt rather disconcerted. I recovered my composure and asked, 'Is she here at the moment?'

'No, sir, she is in Paris, with an artist, a charming boy who loves her, sir, he's passionately in love with her and gives her everything she wants. There, look what she's sent me, to me, her mother. It's good of her, isn't it?'

And with typically southern animation she showed me the big bracelets on her arms and the heavy necklace round her neck. She went on, 'I also have a pair of earrings inset with stones, and a silk dress and some rings, but I don't wear them in the morning,

I only put them on towards evening, when I get dressed up. Oh, she is very happy, sir, very happy. How pleased she will be when I write and tell her you came! But come in, sir, sit down. Naturally you will have something to drink, come in.'

I refused, now wanting to leave by the first train. But she had seized my arm and was drawing me in, repeating, 'Come in then, sir, I have to tell her that you came to our house.'

And I went into a rather dark little room, furnished with a table and a few chairs.

She went on, 'Oh, she is very happy at the moment, very happy. When you met her in the train she was very miserable. Her boyfriend had left her in Marseille. And she was coming home, the poor child. She liked you straight away, but she was still rather sad, you understand. Now she lacks for nothing; she writes and tells me everything she is doing. He is called Monsieur Bellemin. They say he is a great artist in your country. He met her here as he was passing in the street, yes, sir, in the street, and he loved her at once. But of course you will have a glass of *sirop*? It is very good. Are you on your own this year?'

I answered, 'Yes, I am all alone.'

An ever-increasing desire to laugh was creeping up on me as my first disappointment vanished with Madame Rondoli's maternal declarations. I would have to drink a glass of *sirop*.

She was going on, 'What, are you all alone? Oh, how cross I am that Francesca is not here; she would have kept you company as long as you were in town. It's not much fun walking about on your own, and she'll be very sorry too.'

Then, as I was getting up, she cried out, 'But if you would like Carlotta to go with you, she knows all the walks very well. That's my other daughter, sir, the second.'

No doubt she took my amazement for consent and, rushing to

the inner door, she opened it and shouted into the blackness of an invisible staircase, 'Carlotta! Carlotta! Come down quickly, come at once, my dear.'

I wanted to protest; she would hear none of it: 'No, she will keep you company, she is very sweet and much livelier than the other one; she is a good girl, a very good girl, and I love her very much.'

I heard a flop of slipper soles on the steps and a tall girl appeared, dark haired, thin and pretty, but also with unkempt hair, and revealing a young, slim body beneath an old dress of her mother's.

Madame Rondoli at once brought her up to date with my situation. 'It's Francesca's Frenchman, the one from last year, you know. He came to look for her; he is all alone, poor gentleman. So I told him you would go with him to keep him company.'

Carlotta looked at me with her big brown eyes, and she murmured with the beginnings of a smile, 'If that's what he wants, it suits me fine.'

Madame Rondoli pushed her out. 'Go and get dressed, quickly, quickly, put on your blue dress and your hat with the flowers, hurry up.'

As soon as the girl had gone she explained, 'I still have two others, but smaller. It's expensive, you know, bringing up four children! Fortunately the eldest is out of difficulty at the moment.'

And then she told me about her life, about her husband who was dead and had worked on the railways, and about all the qualities of her second daughter Carlotta.

The latter returned, dressed with the same taste as her elder sister, in a garish and rather remarkable dress.

Her mother examined her from head to foot, decided she was quite to her taste, and said to us, 'Off you go now, children.'

172

Then, addressing her daughter, 'Whatever you do, don't come back later than ten o'clock this evening; you know the door will be locked.'

Carlotta replied, 'Don't worry, mamma.'

She took my arm, and there I was wandering through the streets with her just like with her sister the year before.

I returned to the hotel for lunch, then I took my new girlfriend to Santa Margarita, retracing the last outing I had gone on with Francesca.

In the evening she did not go back home, although the door must have been locked after ten o'clock.

And for the two weeks I was able to stay, I took Carlotta round the surroundings of Genoa. She did not cause me to miss her sister.

I took leave of her, full of tears, on the morning of my departure, as I left her, along with a souvenir for herself, four bracelets for her mother.

One of these days I am counting on returning to Italy, as I recall, with a little anxiety mingled with hope, that Madame Rondoli has another two daughters.

'Les Sœurs Rondoli' was first published between 29 May and 5 June 1884 in L'Echo de Paris.

Letter from a Madman

My dear Doctor,

I am putting myself in your hands. Do as you like with me.

I am going to tell you very frankly about my state of mind, and you will evaluate whether it would not be better that I be taken care of for a while in a nursing home, rather than leaving me a prey to the hallucinations and the suffering which are harassing me.

This is the story, in detail and accurate, of the peculiar illness of my mind.

I was living like everybody else, looking at life as humans do, with open, unseeing eyes, without surprise and without understanding. I was living as animals do, as we all do, performing all the functions of existence, examining things and believing I could see, believing I knew, believing I was aware of my surroundings, when one day I noticed that everything was false.

It was a phrase of Montesquieu that suddenly illuminated my thoughts. It is this: 'One organ more or less in our mechanism might have made a different intelligence of us ... In fact all the established laws governing our mechanism in a certain form would be different if our mechanism did not exist in that form.'

I reflected on that passage for months, for months and months, and, little by little, a strange clarity pervaded me, and that clarity brought me into the darkness of night.

It is a fact that our organs are the only intermediaries between the exterior world and ourselves. That is to say that the interior being, which constitutes the self, finds itself in contact with the

174

exterior being which makes up the world by means of a few nerve fibres.

Now, apart from the fact that this exterior being eludes us because of its proportions, its duration, its innumerable and impenetrable properties, its origins, its future or its aims, its distant forms and its infinite manifestations, even as concerns the part of it that we are able to appreciate, our organs only provide us with information that is as uncertain as it is sparse.

Uncertain, because it is only the properties of our sensual organs which determine for us the apparent properties of matter.

Sparse, because our senses being only five in number, the field of their investigations and the nature of their discoveries are very restricted.

I will explain: the eye shows us dimensions, shape and colour; it deceives us on these three points.

It can only reveal to us objects and creatures of average dimensions, in proportion to human size, which has led us to apply the word large to certain things and the word small to certain others, solely because its weakness prevents it from being aware of that which is too big or too small for it. From which it follows that it knows and sees almost nothing, that almost the entire universe remains hidden from it, the star which inhabits space and the animalcule which inhabits a drop of water.

If it even had a hundred million times its normal power, if it could observe in the air which we breathe all the species of invisible creatures, as well as the inhabitants of neighbouring planets, there would still exist infinite numbers of species of smaller animals and worlds so very distant that it could not reach them.

Therefore all our ideas about proportion are false since there is no possible limit to magnitude or smallness.

Our appreciation of dimension and shape has no absolute value, since it is solely determined by the power of an organ and by constant comparison with ourselves.

One may add that the eye is also incapable of seeing transparency. Glass without defects deceives it. It confuses it with the air, which it does not see either.

Let us move on to colour.

Colour exists because our eye is constituted in such a way that it transmits to the brain, in the form of colour, the different ways in which masses absorb and break down the rays of light which fall on them, according to their chemical composition.

The proportions of this absorption and decomposition constitute shades.

So this organ imposes on the mind its way of seeing, or rather its arbitrary fashion of noting dimensions and appreciating the relationships of light with matter.

Let us consider hearing.

Even more than with the eye, we are the playthings and dupes of this fantastic organ.

Two masses colliding produce a certain disturbance of the atmosphere. This movement makes a certain little membrane in our ear quiver, which immediately changes into sound what is, in reality, only a vibration.

Nature is dumb. But the eardrum possesses the miraculous property of transmitting to us in the form of sensations, and the sensations vary according to the number of vibrations and all the tremors of the invisible waves in space.

This metamorphosis produced by the auditory nerve in the short passage from the ear to the brain has allowed us to create a strange art, music, the most poetic and the most precise of the arts, vague as a dream and as accurate as algebra.

What can one say of taste and the sense of smell? Would we

recognize perfumes and quality in food without the bizarre properties of our nose and our palate?

Yet humanity would be able to exist without hearing, without
taste and without a sense of smell; that is to say without any
notion of noise, flavour and scent.

So, if we had a few organs less, we would be ignorant of unusual
and admirable things, but if we had a few organs more, we would
discover around us an infinity of other things which we would
never suspect for lack of the means of observing them.

So, we are mistaken in our judgements of the Known, and we
are surrounded by the unexplored Unknown.

So everything is uncertain and can be appreciated in different
ways.

Everything is false, everything is possible, everything is questionable.

Let us express this certainty by repeating the old saying, 'What
is true on this side of the Pyrenees is false beyond them.'

And let us add: what is true for our organs is false elsewhere.

Two and two ought not to make four any more outside our
atmosphere.

Truth on earth, error beyond, from which I conclude that mysteries of which we have caught a glimpse, such as electricity, hypnosis, telepathy, suggestion, all the phenomena of magnetism,
only remain hidden because nature has not provided us with the
organ, or organs, needed to understand them.

After I had convinced myself that everything revealed to me by
my senses only exists for me as I see it, and would be totally different for another differently organized being, after concluding
that a humanity differently constructed would have ideas
absolutely opposed to ours about the world, about life, about
everything, because agreement about beliefs is only the result of

the similarity of human organs, and divergences in opinion only come from slight differences in the functioning of our nerve fibres, then I made a superhuman effort of thought to speculate about the impenetrability which surrounds me.

Have I gone mad?

I said to myself, 'I am enveloped in the unknown.' I imagined a man without ears who suspects the existence of sound as we suspect so many hidden mysteries, a man recording acoustic phenomena for which he could determine neither the nature nor the source. And I was afraid of everything, all around me, I was afraid of the air, I was afraid of the night. The moment we realize that we can understand almost nothing, and that there are no limits to anything, what remains? A void, is it not? What is there in an apparent void?

This confused terror of the supernatural which has haunted man since the world began is a legitimate terror, since the supernatural is only a name for what remains veiled from us!

Then I understood dread. It seemed to me that I was constantly on the verge of discovering a secret of the universe.

I tried to sharpen the organs of my senses, to excite them, to make them momentarily perceive the invisible.

I said to myself, everything is a being. The cry that passes through the air is a being comparable to an animal since it is born, produces movement, is once more transformed and dies. Thus the fearful mind that believes in incorporeal beings is not mistaken. Who are these beings?

How many men have a presentiment and shiver at their approach, tremble at their indiscernible contact. You feel them near you, around you, but you cannot make them out, for we do not have the eyes to see them, or rather the unknown organ that could discover them.

So, more than anyone, I was feeling them, myself, these supernatural passers by. Beings or mysteries? Do I know? I could not say what they were, but I could always record their presence. And I saw – I saw an invisible creature – as far as one can see such beings.

I would stay motionless for nights on end, sitting at my table, my head in my hands and thinking, thinking of them. Often I thought that an intangible hand, or rather an ungraspable body, had lightly skimmed my hair. It did not touch me, since its essence was not carnal, but weightless, unknowable.

Then one evening I heard my parquet floor creak behind me. It creaked in a peculiar way. I shivered. I turned round. I saw nothing. And I thought no more of it.

But the next day, at the same time, the same noise occurred. I was so frightened that I got up, certain, absolutely certain that I was not alone in my room. Nothing could be seen, though. Everywhere the air was limpid, transparent. My two lamps were illuminating every corner.

The noise did not begin again and little by little I grew calmer; all the same I was still uneasy and turned round frequently.

The next day I shut myself in early, wondering how I could manage to see the Invisible Being that came to visit me.

And I saw it. I nearly died of terror.

I had lit all the candles on the mantelpiece and in my chandelier. The room was lit up as though for a party. My two lamps were burning on my table.

Opposite me was my bed, an old oak bed with columns; to my right the fireplace; to my left the door, which I had bolted; behind me a very big mirrored wardrobe. I was looking at myself in it. I had strange eyes and very dilated pupils.

Then I sat down as I did every day.

The noise had come, the day before and the day before that, at twenty-two minutes past nine. I waited. When the precise moment came, I felt an indescribable sensation, as though a fluid, an irresistible fluid, had penetrated every part of my body, drowning my soul in a terror at once atrocious and benign. And the creaking came, right by me.

As I was turning I got up so quickly that I almost fell. You could see into the mirror as though in broad daylight, yet I could not see myself in it! It was empty, clear, full of light. I was not in it, and yet I was facing. I was looking at it with staring eyes. I did not dare go towards it, knowing that it was between us, it, the Invisible, and that it was hiding me.

Oh, how frightened I was! And then I began to make myself out in a mist deep in the mirror, as though across a stretch of water; and it seemed to me that this water was slipping away from left to right, slowly, so I became more defined from second to second. It was like the end of an eclipse. What was hiding me had no con tours, but a sort of opaque transparence that was lightening bit by bit.

And at last I could make myself out clearly, just as I do every day when I look at myself.

I had seen it!

I have never seen it again.

But I wait for it endlessly, and I feel that my mind is wandering as I wait.

I remain for hours, nights, days, weeks, in front of my mirror, waiting for it! It no longer comes.

It realized that I had seen it. But for myself, I feel I shall wait for it for ever, until I die, I will wait for it without rest, in front of this mirror, like a hunter on the watch.

And in this mirror I am beginning to see mad images, monsters, hideous corpses, all sorts of dreadful animals, atrocious creatures, all the improbable visions that must haunt the mind of madmen.

That is my confession, my dear Doctor. Tell me what I should do.

Certified as a true copy:

Maufrigneuse

'*Lettre d'un fou*' *was first published on 17 February 1885 in* Gil Blas. *It has never previously been translated into English.*

From Paris to Heyst

On the morning of 8 July I receive this telegram: 'Weather fine. Still as predicted. Belgian borders. Equipment and crew leave midday, at head office. Manoeuvres start three p.m. So expect you at factory from five. JOVIS.'

At five o'clock precisely I enter the gas works at La Villette. You might have thought it was the colossal ruin of a town of Cyclops. Enormous dark avenues open up between the heavy gasometers lined up one behind the other like monstrous, truncated columns of different heights, which in times past had perhaps supported some fearful iron edifice.

In the entrance yard lies the balloon, a big pancake of yellow cloth flattened to the ground under a net. They call that the catch in the net, and indeed it does look like a vast fish, caught and dead.

Two or three hundred people are looking at it, sitting or standing around, or else examining the nacelle, a pretty square basket, a basket for human meat bearing on its side golden letters on a mahogany plaque: *Le Horla*.

Suddenly there is a rush, for at last the gas is going into the balloon through a long yellow canvas tube that crawls along the ground, swelling, throbbing like an enormous worm. But another thought, another image strikes all eyes and all minds. This is how nature herself nourishes beings until they are born. The creature that will shortly fly away begins to rise, and as *Le Horla* gets bigger Captain Jovis's helpers stretch out and position the net that covers it so that the pressure remains even and equally distributed at every point.

This operation is very tricky and very important because the resistance of the cotton cloth, so thin, from which the aerostat is made is calculated in relation to the extent of its contact with the closely knit net that will carry the nacelle.

Le Horla was designed by Monsieur Mallet, built under his supervision and by him. Everything has been manufactured in Monsieur Jovis's workshop by the company's own work team, and nothing had been made elsewhere.

Moreover everything is new in this balloon, from the varnish to the valve, those two essentials of ballooning. The cloth must be made impermeable to gas, as the sides of a ship are impermeable to water. The old varnishes based on linseed oil had the double disadvantage of fermenting and of burning the cloth, which would very soon tear like paper.

Valves presented a danger because they might close imperfectly once they had been opened and once the coating with which they were provided, called the poultice, had been broken. Monsieur Lhoste's fall the other week, in the open sea and in the middle of the night, demonstrated the imperfections of the old system.

It can be said that Captain Jovis's two discoveries, principally of the varnish, are of inestimable value to ballooning.

These matters are being discussed in the crowd, and some gentlemen, who seem to be specialists, are declaring authoritatively that we will have come down again before we reach the fortifications.* There is also criticism of many other details of this new design of balloon, which we are about to test with great pleasure and success.

---

* The old fortifications of Paris – so they were not expected to go far!

It is still growing, slowly. Little tears made in transit are being discovered; they are being filled, in the usual way, with pieces of newspaper applied to the cloth and moistened. This method of stopping the holes makes the public anxious and disturbed.

While Captain Jovis and his crew are busy with the last details, the travellers will have dinner in the gas works canteen, as is customary.

When we come out again the balloon is swaying, huge and transparent, a fabulous golden fruit, a fantastic pear, still being ripened by the last rays of the sun as it covers it with flame.

Now the nacelle is being attached, the barometers are being fetched, the siren we will make wail and moan in the night, the two horns as well, and the food supplies, the overcoats, all the small pieces of equipment that this flying basket can fit in, along with the men.

The wind is pushing the balloon on to the gasometers, so it has to be moved away several times to avoid an accident at the start.

All of a sudden Captain Jovis calls the passengers.

Lieutenant Mallet climbs aboard into the aerial net between the basket and the balloon, from where he can watch the progress of *Le Horla* across the sky throughout the night, as the officer of the watch observes the progress of a boat, standing on the bridge.

Monsieur Etienne Beer climbs in next, then Monsieur Paul Bessand, then Monsieur Patrice Eyriès, and then me.

But the balloon is too heavy for the long journey we are to undertake, and Monsieur Eyriès has to give up his place, not without great regret.

Monsieur Jovis, standing on the edge of the basket, requests in very gallant terms that the ladies move away a little, for he is afraid of throwing sand on their hats as he ascends; then he orders, 'Let everything go!' and with a stroke of the knife he cuts the ropes from which hangs the extra ballast all around us to keep us on the ground, and *Le Horla* is free.

In a second we are gone. You feel nothing, you float, you climb, you fly, you soar. Our friends shout and clap, we can scarcely hear them any more, we can only barely see them. We are already so far, so high! What? Have we just left those people down there? Is it possible? Now beneath us Paris spreads out, a dark patch, bluish, criss-crossed by streets from which domes, towers, spires rise here and there; then, all around, the plain, the land intersected by long roads, thin and white in the middle of the green fields, of soft light or dark green, and almost black woods.

The Seine seems like a big curled-up snake, lying motionless, neither head nor tail to be seen; it comes from the distance and goes off in the distance, crossing Paris, and the whole land looks like an immense basin of meadows and forests enclosed on the horizon by a low mountain, far off and circular.

The sun, which can no longer be seen from below, reappears for us, as though it was rising once more, and our balloon itself lights up in this brightness; it must look like a star to those who are watching us. Every second or two, Monsieur Mallet throws a piece of cigarette paper into the void and says quietly, 'We are climbing, we are still climbing,' while Captain Jovis, beaming with joy, rubs his hands as he repeats, 'Well? This varnish, eh, how about this varnish!'

In fact you can only ascertain whether you are climbing or descending by throwing out a piece of cigarette paper from time to time. If this paper, which in reality remains suspended in the air, seems to fall like a stone, then the balloon is climbing; if on the contrary it seems to fly up in the sky, then the balloon is coming down.

The two barometers show about five hundred meters, and we stare in enthusiastic wonderment at the land we are leaving; we are no longer attached to it by anything, and it looks like a painted geographical map, an inordinately large plan of the provinces. Yet all its sounds reach us distinctly, strangely recognizable. You can especially hear the noise of wheels on the roads, the crack of whips, the 'whoa' of carters, the rumbling and whistling of trains, and the laughter of youngsters running around and playing in the squares. Every time we pass over a village it is the children's cries that dominate everything and rise into the sky with the greatest clarity.

Men call out to us; locomotives whistle; we answer with the siren, which utters plaintive, fearful, thin wails, the real voice of a fantastic creature wandering across the world.

From place to place lamps light up, isolated lights in the farms, strings of gaslights in the towns. We are going to the north-west and have glided for a long time over the lake at Enghien. A river is appearing: it is the Oise. So we have a discussion to work out where we are. That town lit up over there, is it Creil or Pontoise? If we were over Pontoise, we should see the junction of the Seine and the Oise; and then that light, that enormous light to the left, is that not the blast furnace of Montataire?

We are in fact over Creil. The spectacle is astonishing; it is night on the earth and we are still in the light, at after ten o'clock. Now we can hear the slight noises of the fields, especially the double cry of quails, then the miaows of cats and the barking of dogs. The dogs certainly sense the balloon, see it and give the alarm. You can hear them, across the whole plain, barking at us and howling, as they howl at the moon. The cattle also seem to wake in their stables, for they low; all the frightened creatures are affected at this aerial monster passing by.

The scents of the earth, too, are rising up to us deliciously, scents of hay, of flowers, of the damp and green earth, perfuming the air, an air so light, so light, so sweet, so delectable that never in my life have I breathed with so much bliss. An unfamiliar, deep well-being has come over me, a well-being of body and mind, made up of feeling carefree, of infinite peace, oblivion, indifference to everything, and this new sensation of traversing space without any of the sensations that make movement intolerable, no noise, no jolting and no vibrations.

Sometimes we are going up and sometimes we are going down. From time to time Lieutenant Mallet, hanging in his spider's web, says to Captain Jovis, 'We are coming down, throw out half a handful.' And the captain, who is talking and laughing with us, a sack of ballast between his knees, takes a little sand from this sack and throws it overboard.

Nothing is more entertaining, more delicate and more fascinating than manoeuvring a balloon. It is a huge plaything, docile and free, which obeys with surprising sensitivity but which is also, and above all, the slave of the wind, over which we have no control.

Throw overboard a pinch of sand, half a newspaper, a few drops of water, the chicken bones we have just eaten, and up it goes abruptly.

The river or the woods we pass over, blowing cold and humid air to us, bring it down by two hundred meters. Over ripe corn it stays level, and over towns it goes up.

The land is sleeping now, or rather men are sleeping on the land, for the awakened animals are still heralding our approach. From time to time the rumbling of a train reaches us, or the whistle of the engine. Over inhabited areas we make the siren moan, and the terrified country people, trembling in their beds, must be asking themselves if it is the angel of the last judgement who is passing by.

But a smell of gas assails us, continuous and strong; we have probably come across a warm current of air and the balloon is inflating, losing its invisible blood through the overflow pipe, called the appendix, which closes itself as soon as the expansion stops.

We are climbing. Now the ground is no longer sending back the echo of our horns; we have already passed six hundred metres. You can't see well enough to consult the instruments, you only know that the pieces of cigarette paper are falling below us like dead butterflies, that we are forever going up, up. You cannot make out the earth any more; light mists separate us from it; and over our heads the population of stars twinkles.

Now a glow is forming ahead of us, a silver glow that makes the sky paler; and suddenly, as though it were rising up from some unknown depths of the lower horizon, the moon appears at the edge of a cloud. It seems to have come from below, while we are looking at it from very high up, leaning on our basket like spectators on a balcony. It draws away from the clouds enveloping it, gleaming and round, and climbs slowly into the sky.

The earth no longer exists, the earth is drowned under a milky vapour that looks like a sea. So we are alone now with the moon, in the immensity of space, and the moon looks like a balloon that is travelling across from us; and our gleaming balloon looks like a bigger moon than the other one, a world wandering across the sky, amid the stars, in the infinite expanse. We are no longer talking, we are no longer thinking, we are no longer living; we are moving, delightfully inert, across space. The air carrying us has made us into beings like itself, mad, joyful and silent beings, intoxicated by this miraculous flight, strangely alert, though motionless. You no longer feel the flesh, no longer feel the bones, no longer feel your heart beat, you have become something inexpressible, birds who don't even have to bother beating their wings.

All memory has vanished from our minds, our thoughts are free from all care, we have no more regrets, plans, hopes. We are looking, we are feeling, we are deliriously enjoying experiencing the pleasure of this fantastic journey; nothing but us and the moon in the sky! We are a nomadic world, a world in motion, like our sisters the planets; and this little world in motion is carrying five men who have left the earth and have already almost forgotten it. You can see now as if it were broad daylight; we are looking at each other in surprise at this brightness, for we only have ourselves and a few clouds floating lower down to look at. The barometers show twelve hundred meters, then thirteen, then fourteen, then fifteen hundred; and the pieces of cigarette paper are still falling around us.

Captain Jovis tells us that the moon has often made aerostats race away like this and that the journey upwards will continue.

We are at two thousand metres now; we are still rising at two thousand three hundred and fifty metres, until at last the balloon stops.

We sound the siren, surprised that no one sends us a reply from the stars.

Presently we are going down, very quickly, and are in no doubt about it; Monsieur Mallet constantly shouts, 'Throw out some ballast, throw out some ballast!' The ballast that we throw into the void, a mixture of sand and stones, comes back into our faces, as if it was coming up again, thrown from below towards the stars, so rapid is our fall.

There is the earth!

Where are we? That upward thrust in the air lasted more than two hours. It is past midnight and we are crossing a big, dry region, well cultivated, full of roads, heavily populated.

There is a town, a large town to the right, another to the left further off. Then, all at once, on the surface of the ground, a brilliant, magical light flickers on and off, then it reappears, then vanishes once more. Jovis, exhilarated by space, exclaims, 'Look, look at the strange effect of the moon on the water. There is no more beautiful sight at night.'

Indeed it is impossible to imagine anything like it, nothing can give any idea of the exceptional brilliance of these discs of bright light which are not fire, do not appear to be reflections, come into being abruptly here or there and go out as quickly.

On winding streams these luminous focal points appear with every turn of the flowing water; but as the balloon is passing as fast as the wind, there is scarcely time to see them.

We are now fairly close to the land, and our friend Beer exclaims, 'Just look! What is that running over there in the field? Isn't it a dog?' Indeed something is running along the ground with remarkable speed, and whatever it is seems to be leaping over ditches, roads, even trees with such ease that we can make no sense of it. The captain laughed: 'It's the shadow of our balloon,' he said. 'It will get bigger as we come down.'

I distinctly hear the loud noise of forges in the distance and, since throughout the night we have not stopped heading towards the Pole star, which I have often watched and consulted from the bridge of my little yacht on the Mediterranean, we are undoubtedly heading towards Belgium.

Our siren and our two horns are sounding without cease. A few cries answer us – a carter pulling to a halt, a drinker out late. We shout, 'Where are we?' But the balloon is going so quickly that the startled man never has time to answer us. The enlarged shadow of *Le Horla*, as big as a child's ball, is speeding before us, over the fields, the roads, the cornfields and the woods. It goes on, on, ahead of us by half a kilometre; and now, leaning out of the basket, I can hear the great noise of wind in the trees and on the crops.

I said to Captain Jovis, 'It's blowing hard!'

He answers, 'No, that's probably falling water.' I insist, sure of my ear, which knows the wind well from hearing it so often whistling in the rigging. Then Jovis nudges my elbow; he is afraid of upsetting his happy and peaceful passengers, for he knows well enough that a storm is chasing us. At last we get a man below to understand us, and he answers, 'Nord.' *

Another hurls the same name at us.

And suddenly a substantial town, judging by the wide spread of its gas lights, appears just in front of us. It is Lille, perhaps. As we approach it, there appears beneath us, all of a sudden, such a surprising eruption of fire that I feel as if I am being carried off to a fabulous land where they make precious stones for giants.

It is a brick works apparently. Here are others, two, three. The molten materials are boiling, throwing out sparks, casting blue, red, yellow and green glares, reflections of monstrous diamonds, rubies, emeralds, turquoises, sapphires, topaz. And nearby the great forges breathe their snorting breath, like the roaring of an apocalyptic lion; the tall chimneys throw their plumes of flame out into the wind, and you can hear the sounds of metal rolling and reverberating, and huge hammers slamming down.

'Where are we?'

---

* The name of the northernmost department of France.

A voice, coming from a joker or someone scared out of their wits, answers:

'In a balloon.'

'Where are we?'

'Lille.'

So we are not wrong. We've already lost sight of the town and Roubaix is over to our right, then well-cultivated, uniform fields, of different shades according to the crop although they look uniformly yellow, grey or brown at night. But the clouds are piling up behind us, covering the moon, while to the east the sky is lightening, becoming pale blue with red reflections. It is dawn. It is coming quickly, now showing us all the little details on the ground, the trains, the streams, the cows, the goats. Everything is passing beneath us with extraordinary speed; there is no time to look, hardly time to notice that other meadows, other fields, other houses have already flown by. The cocks are crowing, but the quacking of ducks dominates everything, as if the world were populated, covered by them, they make so much noise.

Farm workers, up early, wave their arms at us and shout, 'Bring yourselves down.' But we carry on, going neither up nor down, leaning over the edge of the basket and watching the universe flow by under our feet.

Jovis points out another town, very far off. It is coming closer, dominated by ancient bell towers, and enchanting seen like that from on high. We argue. Is it Courtrai? Is it Ghent?

Now we are quite close and we can see that it is surrounded by water and traversed in every direction by canals. Like a Venice of the North. As we pass over the belfry, so close that our drag rope, the long rope hanging under the basket, almost touches it, the Flemish carillon begins to chime three o'clock.

Its quick, light sounds, soft and clear, seems to burst out for us from the thin stone roof we almost brush as we pursue our wandering course. It is a charming good-morning, a friendly good-morning thrown to us by Flanders. We answer with the siren, whose horrid voice resonates through the streets.

It is Bruges; but we have hardly lost sight of it when my neighbour Paul Bessand asks me, 'Isn't there something to the right and ahead of us? It looks like a river.'

Indeed ahead of us a bright line stretches out in the distance, in the clear light of dawn. Yes, it certainly looks like a river, an immense river, with islands in it.

'Let's prepare to descend,' says the captain. He gets Monsieur Mallet, still perched in his net, to come back into the basket; then the barometers and all the hard objects that might hurt us as we are jolted are stowed away.

Monsieur Bessand exclaims, 'Why, there are ship's masts to the left. We have reached the sea.'

The mist has hidden it from us until now. The sea is everywhere, to the left and in front, while to the right the river Escaut, joining the Meuse, stretches out its estuary, vaster than a lake, as far as the sea.

We will have to come down in a minute or two.

The cord of the escape valve, religiously wrapped in a little white cloth bag and placed in full view so that no one would touch it, is unwound and Monsieur Mallet holds it in his hand, while Captain Jovis peers into the distance for a suitable place.

Behind us the thunder rolls. No bird would have taken our crazy course.

'Pull,' cried Jovis.

We are passing over a canal. The basket shudders twice and

then leans over. The drag rope has touched the big trees on both banks.

But we are going so fast that the long trailing rope does not seem to slow us down now, and we are heading at the speed of a bullet for a big farm; terrified chickens, pigeons and ducks fly about in all directions, while calves, cats and dogs rush, bewildered, towards the house.

We have just half a sack of ballast left. Jovis throws it out, and *Le Horla* flies just over the roof.

'The valve!' cries the captain once more.

Monsieur Mallet hangs on to the cord and we come down like an arrow.

With a stroke of the knife the retaining rope round the anchor is cut; we trail it behind us in a big field of beetroots.

Here come the trees.

'Careful! Hang on! Mind your heads!'

Again we pass over them; then a big jolt buffets us. The anchor has bitten.

'Careful! Hold tight! Hold yourself up with all the strength in your wrists. We are going to touch down.'

The basket does indeed touch the earth. And then flies off again. It falls back again, bounds up and, at last, settles on the ground, while the balloon flails about crazily, in a last dying effort.

The farm workers come running up but do not dare to come too close. They take a long time making up their minds before they come over to release us, for you cannot get a foot to the ground until the balloon is almost completely deflated.

At the same time as the frightened men come over, some of whom are jumping up and down in astonishment and gesticulating like savages, all the cows that have been grazing on the dunes advance towards us, surrounding our balloon with a strange and comical circle of horns, big eyes and snorting nostrils.

With the help of the obliging and hospitable Belgian farmers we manage to pack up our equipment in a very short time and to carry it to Heyst railway station, where we plan to catch the train to Paris at twenty past eight.

The descent has taken place at three fifteen in the morning, only a few seconds ahead of the torrential rain and blinding lightning of the storm that has chased us before it.

Thus, thanks to Captain Jovis, whose daring has long ago been reported to me by my colleague Paul Ginisty, as they fell deliberately into the open sea together off Menton, thus we have been able to see in a single night from high up in the sky the sun setting, the moon rising and the return of day, and to travel from Paris to the Escaut estuary through the air.

'De Paris à Heyst' was first published in Le Figaro *on 16 July 1887. It has never before been translated into English.*

The Donkey

Not a breath of air was passing through the thick mist sleeping over the river. It was like a dull cotton cloud laid upon the water. The banks themselves were still indistinct, hidden under weird vapours festooned like mountains. But the hillside was starting to become visible as daybreak approached. In the growing glow of the dawn, big white blotches that were plaster-clad houses were appearing little by little at its foot. Some cocks were crowing in chicken sheds.

Over there, on the other side of the river, buried beneath the fog, just opposite La Frette, a slight noise now and again disturbed the great silence of the windless sky. Sometimes it was a vague slapping, like the careful progress of a boat, sometimes a sharp blow like an oar hitting planking, sometimes a soft object falling into the water. Then nothing.

Sometimes murmured words would slip by, coming from who knew where, perhaps from far off, perhaps very close, wandering in the opaque mists that had risen from the earth or the river, and then pass on, timid too, like wild birds who have slept in the reeds and leave as the first pale light shows in the sky, to flee again, to flee for ever, glimpsing for a second crossing the mist with out-spread wings, calling with a gentle and fearful cry that wakes their brothers all along the banks.

Suddenly, near the riverside, close by the village, a shadow appeared on the water. At first it was scarcely visible, then it got bigger, became more pronounced, and out of the nebulous curtain thrown over the river a flat-bottomed boat with two men on board ran aground against the grass.

The one who was rowing got up and took a bucket full of fish from the bottom of the craft; then he flung the still glistening net over his shoulder. His companion, who had not moved, spoke: 'Bring your gun. We'll go and knock off a rabbit on the bank, eh, Mailloche?'

The other answered, 'All right by me. Wait, I'm coming.'

And he went off to put their catch somewhere safe.

The man who had stayed in the boat slowly filled his pipe and lit it.

His name was Labouise, though he was called Chicot, and he had formed a partnership with his crony Maillochon, commonly called Mailloche, to carry on the vague and shady occupation of scavengers.

Bargemen in a small way, they would only work at that regularly in the months when they were short. The rest of the time they would be scavenging. Prowling about day and night on the river, scouting for any prey dead or alive, water poachers, nocturnal hunters, a kind of sewer skimmer, sometimes on the lookout for deer in the forest of Saint-Germain, sometimes emptying the pockets of drowned bodies as they slipped away under the water, collectors of floating rags or empty bottles carried along with the current and swaying drunkenly with their mouths in the air, or pieces of driftwood – Labouise and Maillochon took life easy.

Now and again they would leave towards midday on foot, and would go off wandering as the mood took them. They would eat in some inn at the riverside and leave again side by side. They would be gone a day or two, then one morning you would see them again prowling about in the muck heap which served as their boat.

Somewhere, at Joinville or Nogent, distressed oarsmen would

be searching for their craft, which had disappeared one night, untied and gone, no doubt stolen; while twenty or thirty leagues away, on the river Oise, a bourgeois landowner would be rubbing his hands as he admired the dinghy he'd bought second hand the day before for fifty francs from two men who had sold it to him, just like that, in passing, having spontaneously suggested it when they caught sight of him.

Maillochon reappeared with his gun wrapped in a rag. He was a man of forty or fifty, tall, thin, with the alert eyes of people plagued by legitimate worries and of animals that are often hunted. His open shirt revealed a hairy chest like grey fleece. But he seemed never to have had any beard other than a short brush-like moustache and a pinch of stiff hairs beneath his lower lip. He was bald at the temples.

When he lifted the cake of dirt which served as a cap, his scalp seemed to be covered with a misty down, a shadow of hair, like the body of a plucked chicken that is about to be singed.

Chicot, on the other hand, was red and spotty, short, fat and hairy, and looked like a raw beefsteak hidden in a sapper's fur helmet. He kept his left eye permanently closed as though he was aiming at something or someone, and when people joked about this tic, shouting to him, 'Open your eye, Labouise,' he would calmly reply, 'Never fear, gorgeous, I opens it when I needs.' In fact he was in the habit of calling everyone 'gorgeous', even his scavenging companion.

He took his turn at the oars, and once more the craft plunged into the mist, hanging motionless over the river but becoming white like milk as the sky lit up with a rosy glow.

Labouise asked, 'What yer bring for shot, Maillochon?'

Maillochon answered, 'A little 'un, nine, that's what we wants for rabbit.'

They were approaching the other bank so slowly, so gently, that no sound gave them away. This bank belongs to the forest of Saint-Germain and rabbit shooting is restricted. It is covered in rabbit warrens hidden among the tree roots, and at dawn the animals frisk about, to and fro, coming in and going out.

Maillochon, on his knees in the bow, was on the lookout, the gun hidden in the bottom of the boat. Suddenly he grabbed it, aimed, and the report resounded for some time through the calm countryside.

With two strokes of the oar, Labouise touched the bank and his companion jumped ashore and picked up a little grey rabbit, still quivering.

Then the boat plunged into the fog once more to get to the other bank and out of reach of the keepers.

The two men seemed now to be moving gently along in the water. The weapon had disappeared under the plank which served as a hiding place, and the rabbit was tucked into Chicot's baggy shirt.

After a quarter of an hour Labouise said, 'Come on, gorgeous, time for another one.'

Maillochon answered, 'Suits me. Off we go.'

And the boat set off again, going quickly downstream. The mists covering the river were beginning to lift. As if through a veil you could make out the trees on the banks, and the dissipating fog was floating off with the current in little clouds.

As they approached the island that has its point opposite Herblay, the two men slowed down and began to watch out again. A second rabbit was soon shot.

After that they went on downstream until they were half way to Conflans, then they stopped, moored their boat to a tree and, lying in the bottom, went to sleep.

From time to time Labouise would prop himself up and scan the skyline with his open eye. The last morning vapours had evaporated and the big summer sun was climbing, radiant, into the blue sky.

Over on the other side of the river the vine-covered hillside curved in a semi-circle. A single house stood at the top in a grove of trees. Everything was silent.

But on the towpath something was moving gently, hardly making any progress. It was a woman pulling a donkey. The arthritic animal, stiff and stubborn, would stretch out a leg from time to time, yielding to the efforts of its companion when it could refuse no longer; it was going along in that fashion with its neck thrust out, ears flattened, so slowly that it was impossible to calculate when it would be out of sight.

The woman was pulling, bent double, and coming back sometimes to hit the donkey with a branch.

Labouise, noticing it, said, 'Eh-up, Mailloche.'

Mailloche replied, 'What is it?'

'Want a laugh?'

'Too right.'

'Go on, shake a leg, gorgeous, and us'll laugh.'

Chicot took up the oars.

When he had crossed the river and was opposite the pair, he cried, 'Eh-up, gorgeous!'

The woman stopped pulling her jenny and looked.

Labouise went on, 'On your way to a traction engine fair?'

The woman did not answer. Chicot continued, 'Hey, that there's a racing model, is your donk. Where you taking it at such a lick?'

The woman, at last, replied, 'I'm going to Macquart, in Champioux, to have it slaughtered. It's no good any more.'

Labouise replied, 'I'll say. And what'll Macquart give you for it?'

The woman, who was wiping her brow with the back of her hand, hesitated. 'How should I know? Maybe three francs, maybe four.'

Chicot cried out, 'I'll give you a hundred sous and there's your race done, that's worth a bit.'

After brief reflection, the woman announced, 'Done.'

And the scavengers climbed ashore.

Labouise seized the animal's bridle. Maillochon asked in astonishment, 'What'll you do with that heap?'

This time Chicot opened his other eye to show his mirth. The whole of his red face was contorted with joy; he chortled, 'Never fear, gorgeous, I got my ideas.'

He gave a hundred sous to the woman, who sat down by the ditch to see what would happen.

Then Labouise, in fine humour, went to look for the gun and held it out to Maillochon.

'We takes turns, my old girl; we'll hunt big game, gorgeous – not that close, dang it, you'll kill it first go. Got to make the fun last a bit.'

And he planted his companion forty paces from the victim. The donkey, noticing it was free, was trying to graze on the tall grass on the riverbank, but it was so exhausted that it wobbled on its legs as if it was about to fall.

Maillochon slowly took aim and said, 'Bit of salt on its ears, watch, Chicot.'

And he fired a shot.

The tiny pellets spattered the donkey's long ears, and it began to shake them vigorously, first one, then the other, then together, to get rid of the stinging.

The two men were splitting their sides laughing, bent double, stamping their feet. But the indignant woman leapt up, not wanting her jenny martyred, offering to give back the hundred sous, furious and complaining.

Labouise threatened her with a leathering and made as if to roll his sleeves up. He'd paid, hadn't he? Then shut it. He'd give her one up the skirt to show her you didn't feel a thing.

She went off threatening them with the police. They heard her for a long time shouting insults that became more violent as she got further away.

Maillochon held the gun out to his mate.

'Your go, Chicot.'

Labouise took aim and fired. The donkey took the blast on the rump, but the lead shot was so small and came from such a distance that no doubt it thought it had been bitten by horseflies. It began to whisk them away hard with its tail, beating its legs and back.

Labouise sat down to laugh in comfort, while Maillochon reloaded the gun so merrily that he seemed to be sneezing into the barrel.

He came a few paces nearer and, aiming at the same spot as his mate, shot once more. This time the animal gave a leap, tried to kick, and turned its head. A little blood was flowing at last. The shot had gone in deep, and it was beginning to feel sharp pain, for it began to run away along the bank at a slow, limping, jerky gallop.

The two men rushed off in pursuit, Maillochon with great strides, Labouise with hurried steps, running with a small man's breathless trot.

But the donkey had stopped, its strength exhausted, and with a look of desperation was watching the murderers approach. Then, all at once, it stretched out its head and began to bray.

Labouise, panting, had taken the gun. This time he came quite close, not wanting to start the chase again.

When the ass had finished uttering its pitiful complaint, like a call for help, a last impotent cry, the man had an idea and shouted out, 'Mailloche, hey! Gorgeous, come on, I'm going to make it take its medicine.' And while the other forced open the animal's clenched jaws, Chicot pushed the barrel of his gun right down into its gullet, as if he wanted to make it drink some medicine; then he said, 'Hey, gorgeous, watch out, here comes the purge.'

And he pulled the trigger. The donkey took three steps back, fell on its behind, tried to get up and collapsed at last on its side as it closed its eyes. The whole of its old, bare body was quivering; its legs were moving as though it wanted to run. A stream of blood was flowing between its teeth. Soon it stopped moving. It was dead.

The two men were not laughing; it was over too quickly, they had been robbed.

Maillochon asked, 'Well, what's to do now?'

'Never fear, gorgeous, let's load it up, us'll laugh come nightfall.'

And they went to look for the boat. The animal's body was laid in the bottom and covered with fresh grass, and the two prowlers stretched out on top and went to sleep.

Towards midday Labouise took a litre of wine, a loaf of bread, butter and some raw onions out of the secret lockers of their muddy and worm-eaten boat, and they began to eat.

When they had finished their meal they lay down once more on the dead donkey and went to sleep again. At nightfall Labouise woke up and, shaking his mate who was snoring like a barrel organ, ordered, 'Come on, gorgeous, off we go.'

Maillochon began to row. They went back up the Seine at quite a gentle pace, since they had plenty of time. They passed banks covered with flowering water irises and perfumed with hawthorns that dangled bunches of white blossom over the flowing water; and the heavy, mud-coloured boat slid over the big flat leaves of water lilies, bending over their pale, round flowers, split like bells, which came upright again after they had passed.

When they got to the wall at Eperon, which separates the forest of Saint-Germain from Maisons-Laffitte park, Labouise stopped his mate and explained his plan, sending Maillochon into convulsions of silent and prolonged laughter.

They threw the grass spread out over the dead body into the water, took the animal by the feet, got it ashore and hid it in a thicket.

Then they climbed back in their boat and made for Maisons-Laffitte.

The night was completely black when they entered the premises of Père Jules, caterer and café owner. As soon as he saw them the trader came up, shook their hands and sat down at their table, and they talked of one thing and another.

Towards eleven o'clock, the last customer having gone, Père Jules winked and said to Labouise, 'Well, is there any?'

Labouise made a movement with his head and announced, 'There is and there isn't, you never know.'

The restaurant owner persisted. 'Grey ones, just grey ones maybe?'

Then Chicot plunged his hand into his woollen shirt, pulled out the ears of a rabbit and declared, 'That's worth three francs the pair.'

Then there was a long discussion over the price. They agreed on two francs sixty-five. And the two rabbits were handed over.

As the two marauders rose to leave, Père Jules, who was watching them, remarked, 'You've got something else, but you don't want to say so.'

Labouise retorted, 'Could be, but not for you, you're too stingy.'

The trader, his interest aroused, pressed him.

'Hmm, something big. Go on, say what. We can agree terms.'

Labouise, who seemed puzzled, made as if to question Maillochon with a look, then answered slowly, 'Here's how it is. I'm laid up by Eperon when summat passes us in the first bush to the left, at the end of the wall. Mailloche lets off a shot, it goes down. And we makes off, on account of the keepers. I can't say what it be, seeing as how I don't know. It's big, right enough. But what? If I told you what I wouldn't be straight, and you knows, gorgeous, between us, cross my heart.'

The man, in suspense, asked, 'It ain't a deer?'

Labouise went on, 'Could easily be, that or summat else. A deer? … Yes … Perhaps 'tis bigger. You could say a doe. Oh, I don't say as how it is a doe, seeing as I don't know, but it could be!'

The cook-house owner persisted, 'Mebbe a stag?'

Labouise stretched out his hand. 'Oh, no! As to a stag, it's not a stag, I'll be straight with you, it's not a stag. I would've seen him, seeing as how it's woods. No, that be no stag.'

'Why didn't you take it with you?' the man asked.

'Why, gorgeous? Because we'll be selling on the spot from now on. I've a taker. You knows how it is, you goes and wanders about in there, you finds something, you gets hold of it. No risks for yours truly. That's it.'

The cook said suspiciously, 'Suppose he's not there any more?'

But Labouise raised his hand again. 'As to being there, he be there, I promise, I swear it. In the first spinney on the left. As to what it be, I don't know. I know it's not a stag, that, no, I'm sure of that. As to anything else, it's for you to go and see. It's twenty francs where it lies. Suit you?'

The man was still hesitating. 'You wouldn't bring it to me?'

Maillochon took over: 'There's no gamble in that. If it be a deer, fifty francs; if it be a doe, seventy; them's our prices.'

The cook-house owner made up his mind. 'Done for twenty francs. Put it there.' And they shook hands on it.

Then he took from behind his counter four big hundred sou coins, which the two friends pocketed.

Labouise got up, emptied his glass and went out; as he was about to disappear into the shadows he turned round and said firmly: 'It's no stag, for sure. But what? ... As to being there, it be there. Give you back your money if you find nothing.'

And he plunged into the night.

Maillochon, who was following him, slapped him on the back with great thumps of his fist to express his delight.

'L'Ane' was first published on 15 July 1883 in Le Gaulois.

Chronology

1850 5th August, birth of Guy de Maupassant in the Château de Miromesnil near Dieppe, the residence of his parents (Laure and Gustave de Maupassant) from 1849 to 1853.

1856 Birth of Maupassant's younger brother Hervé in the Château d'Ymauville, Grainville-Ymauville, (described by Maupassant in *Une Vie*), where the family lived from 1854 to 1859. Many holidays were spent with Maupassant's maternal grandmother, Mme Le Poittevin, at the nearby fishing port of Fécamp.

1858 The family spent the summer by the sea at Etretat and began buying parcels of land there, on which they built a house; Etretat, then a simple fishing village, was fast becoming a fashionable holiday resort.

1859 Maupassant went to school in Paris (Lycée Napoléon, now Henri IV) for the academic year 1859–60 only; it is not clear why he did not stay there. During this period the family left Ymauville to live in the house in Etretat.

1862 At the beginning of this year Maupassant's parents separated, his father living in Paris and his mother in Etretat with the two boys; apart from the one year of school above, Mme de Maupassant had taught her sons herself and was well able to do so as she was an intelligent, cultivated and educated woman. The separation (they never divorced) seemed a reasonably amicable one, but Maupassant saw little of his father in his adolescence. He spent much of his free time with the local fishermen.

1863 In October Maupassant went as a boarder to the Institution Ecclésiastique in Yvetot, not far away, a Catholic religious foundation noted for its excellence in Classics; he did not enjoy the lack of freedom, sometimes feigning illness as a means of escape.

1864 He was saving for a boat – one like the local fishing boats.

1866 Maupassant left Yvetot, ostensibly owing to a difference of opinion between his mother and the Superior concerning fasting in Lent. In April he went to the Lycée in Le Havre for only two weeks, then appeared to stay at home, returning to Yvetot in October for the new school year; in spite of this disruption he still did well at school.

1868 In May he was expelled from Yvetot for expressing anti-religious sentiments. He was sent at once to the Lycée in Rouen, where he soon made contact with Louis Bouilhet, poet, dramatist, town librarian, Flaubert's friend and known to Maupassant's family; Maupassant had been writing poetry for some years. At home in Etretat he met another poet, Swinburne, who on 18 September had been dramatically rescued from drowning while staying with his friend George Powell; Maupassant had gone to the rescue but another fishing boat picked Swinburne up. Powell, a Welsh eccentric who had just bought a cottage in Etretat and was already slightly known to Maupassant, invited him to several bizarre lunches. Back at school in Rouen that winter, he saw Bouilhet regularly and sometimes Flaubert too, but Maupassant did not know Flaubert well at that stage.

1869 Bouilhet died unexpectedly, Maupassant passed the Baccalauréat examination soon after, and school days were over. He registered for the first year of law in Paris.

1870 His law studies were interrupted by the outbreak of the Franco-Prussian war in July; he volunteered. Little is known of his movements during the war, though he was involved in the retreat of the French before the rapid Prussian advance on Rouen in December 1870. He was demobilized in late 1871. His father 'bought' a man to replace him, the only way to avoid serving a total of seven years in the army.

1872 Maupassant entered the Marine Ministry as a supernumerary, He achieved a permanent paid post in 1873 and stayed in the Ministry until 1878.

1873 He began to see a great deal of Flaubert, showing him his early attempts at writing, at first poetry, then prose. Their relationship developed for seven years, at first as a literary apprenticeship, then a close friendship. From 1872 on Maupassant's parallel activities on the river, with rowing-boats and girls, were pursued with vigour, intensity and enthusiasm. He always owned or part-owned a boat, sometimes several.

1875   Published his first story under a pseudonym in a provincial paper, and was also writing two plays (one an obscene comedy for private performance) and a story, 'Dr Heraclius Gloss' – none of them published in his lifetime.

1876   Finished another play and had some poems published, and also published two articles and a story. He had met many writers through Flaubert's Sunday afternoons – Zola, Turgenev, Alphonse Daudet, Edmond de Goncourt and the young Henry James. He began to see regularly what would later become the Médan group – Alexis, Céard, Hennique, Huysmans. By 1876 he also undoubtedly had syphilis, and from then on he had to live with very variable periods of illness or disability. The disease accompanied his literary career, like an increasingly intrusive shadow, to its end.

1878   Maupassant had been very unhappy at the Marine Ministry and, with Flaubert's help, managed to transfer to the Ministry responsible for Fine Arts and Education. He published two more stories and started his first novel, *Une Vie*, but had to put it aside for a few years.

1879   His play, *Histoire du vieux temps*, a one-act comedy, was successfully performed at the Théâtre Déjazet. Another story was published, he began writing 'Boule de suif' and had a poem published for which he was prosecuted for 'outrage to public morality'; the case was later dismissed, thanks once more to Flaubert's help.

1880   A book of poems was published, *Des vers*, which was well received, and 'Boule de suif' appeared in the collection *Les Soirées de Médan*, completely overshadowing the other stories by Alexis, Céard, Hennique, Huysmans and Zola; Maupassant had arrived. At the same time as his sudden fame came the severe blow of the death of Flaubert, who had become a kind of father figure to the younger man. Maupassant was now on his own and his life changed. He began to write regularly for the newspaper *Le Gaulois*, and his first story was 'Les Dimanches d'un bourgeois de Paris'. At the same time he took extended temporary leave from the Ministry (which became permanent eighteen months later), and the stories and articles began to pour out in an ever-increasing flood.

1881   He went to Algeria for three months for *Le Gaulois* and on his return began to write for *Gil Blas* as well, also writing occasionally for other papers and magazines. He published his first collection of stories under the title of one of them, *La Maison tellier*, a pattern which he followed through thirteen such collections.

1883   Maupassant now published his first novel, *Une Vie*, had his own house, 'La Guillette', built in Etretat, and at the end of the year employed a valet, François Tassart, who remained with him to the end of his life.

1884   Published his first travel book, *Au soleil*, partly based on his time in Algeria for *Le Gaulois*. 'Les Soeurs Rondoli' appeared, first in a newspaper then as the title story of his sixth collection.

1885   Published his second novel, *Bel-Ami*; he was thought to have produced unflattering portraits of actual journalists and newspaper proprietors, a charge he denied. He had ceased to write regularly for *Le Gaulois* before publication of the book, but continued with *Gil Blas*.

1886   Published his third novel, *Mont-Oriol*. Set in the Auvergne, it is a rather bitter love story involved with capitalist speculation in the creation of a new spa, and with a comic and highly cynical view of medicine. In October Maupassant bought an eleven-metre boat, the *Audacieux* (previously *Flamberge*), renaming her *Bel-Ami*, and went on many short Mediterranean cruises that winter and the following spring.

1888   The fourth novel, *Pierre et Jean*, appeared together with his study on the novel, *Le Roman*. The novel was first serialized (late 1887), and *Le Roman* was first published separately in *Le Figaro*; this led to a lawsuit as the newspaper made cuts which rendered part of the essay nonsensical. *Sur l'eau* appeared, and the short stories continued, but their hectic pace was slowing.

1889   Published his fifth novel, *Fort comme la mort*, which dealt with the society he now moved in and finely analysed the process of ageing. Maupassant's brother Hervé died, insane, in November, at the age of thirty-three. One can see now that he must have died of syphilis, but the link between that form of insanity and syphilis was then only beginning to be suspected. Hervé's widow and small daughter were now dependent on Maupassant, who found himself very stretched financially.

1890   Publication of *La Vie errante*, his third travel book, and *L'Inutile Beauté*, his last collection of stories. Maupassant's last novel, *Notre cœur*, about the impossibility of love in Parisian high society, was also published in this year. He started two further novels, neither of which he was able to finish, and planned articles which were never written. He published nothing new after 1890.

1891 Maupassant now had very serious health worries. The physical problems worsened, and increasingly he had mental difficulties as well. He moved despairingly from place to place, consulting innumerable doctors.

1892 On 1 January, in Cannes, he made a failed suicide attempt; it was no longer possible to conceal the fact that he had General Paralysis of the Insane (one of the manifestations of the third stage of syphilis), and he was transferred to a clinic in Paris, becoming more and more demented.

1893 He died on 6 July, a month before his forty-third birthday.

Short Bibliography and Translation Notes

Anon., 'Monsieur Dumollet' (song sheet), Paris, Ancienne Maison Quantin, 1891

Barbier, Pierre, *Histoires de France par les chansons*, Vol. 7, Gallimard, 1959, pp. 189–191

Bienvenu, Jacques, *Maupassant inédite*, Aix-en-Provence, Edisud, 1993

Forestier, Louis, 'Maupassant et l'Italie', in *Maupassant multiple*, Toulouse, Presses Universitaires du Mirail, 1995

Maupassant, Guy de, *Contes et nouvelles*, Paris, La Pléiade, Gallimard, 1974, 1979

— *Les Dimanches d'un bourgeois de Paris*, Paris, Sedes, 1989, notes by Louis Forestier. I cannot adequately express how valuable Louis Forestier's notes in this and the above edition have been

— *Chroniques*, Paris, UGE, 10/18, 1980. This edition is not complete

Tassart, François, *Souvenirs sur Guy de Maupassant*, Paris, Plon, 1911

— *Nouveaux Souvenirs intimes*, Paris, Nizet, 1962

Maupassant wrote about 306 stories (some are difficult to classify as story or article), of which less than a third have had good, modern translations – not all currently in print – and only about 130 are in print at all. Some old translations are still in print, but they vary from the good but slightly dated to the unacceptable. However good they were, any hint of eroticism was either omitted or toned down; sometimes several lines are missing altogether, sometimes only a word or two has been altered, but Maupassant's intention has been changed. His simplicity of style too has often been obscured; his prose was spare, carefully chosen, and even his flights of lyricism have a certain strictness and restraint. It is a pity that, while Flaubert's style was respected in translation, this has not always been so for Maupassant, and more modern translations are needed.

The most widely distributed Maupassant translations can be traced back to two sources published during the 1920s: Marjorie Laurie (London, Werner Laurie) and Ernest Boyd and Storm Jameson (New York, Knopf), and both publishers produced what purported to be complete collections. These have long been out of print in England (except for a small number of stories), but several editions are still available in the USA (Knopf and another even older one first published by Black in 1903).

In the USA there was also *The Complete Short Stories* (New York, Hanover House, 1955), edited by the respected Maupassant specialist Artine Artinian and containing some stories not in other editions, one of which appears in this book. Most are reprints of the Boyd and Jameson translations, just one was newly translated by Francis Steegmuller, and the rest are anonymous. Many of these anonymous translations are a travesty, with some appalling mistakes which would be risible if not even more lamentable, and in one case even omitting fully half of the story. For practical purposes I have disregarded the anonymous translations.